41

The Symbol of Hate

by Muhammad Irtiza Mehdi Bangash

Copyright © 2023 Muhammad Irtiza Mehdi
All rights reserved.
ISBN: 9798395726537

Table of Contents
I   Pg#5
PART I   Pg#7
1   Pg#8
2   Pg#17
3   Pg#28
4   Pg#39
5   Pg#51
6   Pg#63
7   Pg#74
8   Pg#86
9   Pg#103
10 Pg#111
11 Pg#123
12 Pg#131
13 Pg#140
14 Pg#147
15 Pg#156
16 Pg#165
PART II   Pg#176
A DUE APOLOGY & TRAIL OF REGRETS   Pg#177
THE REPLY TO HIS 'WHY?' Pg#186
THE FINALE OF THE TALE Pg#198
PART III   Pg#214
THE SEVEN SYMBOLS   Pg#215

I

The street was gloomy. The night was unusually cold. Everything was still, as this day was going to be a decisive one for a family. Even the owls didn't stay awake, wolves didn't howl, but the cold wind did its job. A woman tried to walk briskly in the street, but every step proved to be more and more difficult for her. She finally reached the door and knocked it. Her trembling hands didn't make enough sound. She knocked again.

After getting no response, she was determined that no one lived there. As she whirled around, someone opened the door. She could feel the heaviness around her; she could feel someone breathing rapidly behind her. She turned. Her heart stopped beating for a moment. A man in his late 20s was standing in front of her.

"Vernon, is it you?" she inquired hesitantly.

He didn't reply. He just started moving backwards. He leapt to his feet before the woman could say anything else. His face was expressionless as if he was indifferent to the events going around him. He entered the kitchen with all his might. The woman followed him. He took a sharp knife from the drawer.

> "Stop! You will cause havoc to the family!" she uttered these words while her lips went heavy. Tears were trickling down her cheeks.
> "Which family?" questioned his eyes.

There was some silence for a minute. They were compelled to hear the sound of the roaring wind that announced the end of this tale. Vernon kept looking down for some moments, and then looked into her eyes. He uttered only one word and repeated it thrice,

> "Why? Why? Why?"

A shriek followed this painful quiver. The clouds burst with a cry as if the trumpet was finally blown. The war between love and hatred met a temporary end.

PART-I

1

(If anyone is reading the diary, I want you to understand the way I wrote it. Spaces before any paragraph lead the reader to a different part of the day in this account. Paras with no space show that the flow of thoughts is uninterrupted up till then)

I wanted to revise the vocabulary which I learned from Aunt Jessica's library. I needed to check whether my writing was the same as it used to be when I and Stephen would grab the leather diary (for which we spent our two months' pocket money), and would write things in it. These last few years have been tough, but some good things have happened too. As it's our 4th anniversary, what can be more special? I am trying my best to write down everything hastily so that whenever someone finds this diary, he/she could feel the rawness.

Things aren't the same now, and I have become

more wrecked. It seems as if everything has slowly floated away in the acrid cloud of time. I've just lived a quarter of my life but it feels as if I'm older than the granny living next to the Onerwaarten's famous park. I feel guilty too for unnecessarily dragging Willa into my problems.

She isn't willing to go out for our anniversary special dinner, and I fully understand her, as the never-ending battle going on within the enclosed walls of her head is enough to make someone spiritually dead. She is emotionally unstable. I am trying my best to make Willa believe that she is the best thing that has ever happened to me. The softness in her behavior has no match, and her beauty is equally charismatic. After my mother, she is the second most elegant woman I have ever seen. I can't forget the day when we signed the paper to get our love a name.

The day extracted the essence from all the love chunks that keep the casket of goodness intact. The day commenced with romantic weather. Chirping birds were whispering their love rhymes in my ears. The hearts of the invitees were getting drenched in the potion of love, and the mist from it was melting away even the slightest of impurity plaguing their hearts. The events of my wedding were so surreal that it was becoming difficult for me to ignore the fact that the veil between all the realms had been brought down, leading to a free mixing of all the creatures of the universe.

15th November was an unforgettable day. Willa's tight-fitting and utterly stylish clothes were in no match with the grace she was adorning, but still, a green attire that epitomized her ultimate grace. The perfection was amplified by the diamonds that were used to grant the dress some charm. It's the only thing that I remember, and I want to remember.

The last 4 years have been precious but the most painful ones too. Paying tribute to her for how she has handled me is important. She taught me to talk again, she made me walk again, and she helped heal my wounds. I am looking forward to the day when everything will get back to normal. I am waiting for the day when she will get what she deserves. She has gained nothing, as for now, but it can't be any less true that even if I have to serve her as a slave, I won't be able to pay off the sacrifices she has made for me. She was the only person who wept my tears, and kept my crippling body intact after I lost someone like Dad. Dad's death had sucked out all the colors that once used to fill my life, but Willa was that flower whose aroma draped my heart to pacify it, and the quilt of love that she had lent me, made me feel spiritually warmer.

As words fall short to describe how great of a blessing Willa is, I just want her to know that I want to make her life even more beautiful than she has made mine. I have been trying to convince her for a candlelight dinner, but the worries creeping into her fragile heart are stopping her from opting for it.

"I promise, there is going to be only you and me."
"You remember what happened last time, right?" she questioned rhetorically, while her still eyes kept staring at my soul.
"Oh, just forget it. It was just a strange thought ruining our memories."
"Why do you all want to prove that I have gone insane?"
"Oh, darling, who called you that? OK, just relax! We aren't going anywhere. I am bringing your medicine."
"I don't want anything! Just get me something to kill me."

Whenever she talks about dying, I feel destitute. I think this uncalled-for partner that is haunting her life, is going to stay with us forever. Why do I hate things starting with the alphabet 'S' (except my childhood best friend Stephen)? Schizophrenia has to be the worst of the disorders. As far as Stephen is concerned, I have been looking at the door of his house since he left, but he never came back after going on a trip to his grandparent's home. It breaks my heart to see how some close relations turn so anonymous.

For the past few hours, I have been searching for

some ways to make a schizophrenia patient happy, but couldn't find anything useful. I was thinking of getting Willa some roses by the time she leaves her bed. Planning to roast a turkey too, but I'm going to start cooking a bit late as I gave Willa her meds, and she won't get ready until she gets done with the petrifying hallucinations. She suffers from severe diarrhea after her dosage and vomits profusely, so I've to go for a light dinner. I also searched for some decoration ideas and went with the ones that matched my expectations.

I just washed the dishes and as usual, Willa didn't eat anything, although the memories that we made at the dinner are going to stick with me for quite some time. Willa looked stunning. She wore a purple cotton shirt with a dramatic skirt concealing her delicate waist. She chose the perfume which I gave her on our first anniversary, the very same perfume that my mother used to apply. The smell itself played an essential role in popping the bubble holding all the memories of my childhood. Those roses stuck in her braid were complimenting her appearance. Her comely face never requires makeup, but her hazel contacts were dazzling like some never seen stars in the sky. The odor of her hair was making me want to love her more. I can't find more words to describe her bewitching beauty, and maybe I will need to consult a dictionary to do that.

She just took a small bite out of the incredibly tender turkey. After the dinner, we laid the mat that kept reminding us of its culturally deep-rooted significance whenever we would roll over it. We slept supine, counting the stars and following the moving ones crossing our gaze with our eyes. However, there has to be something unexpected that stops you from making memories, and this time it took our intimate moments in its wrath by taking the form of a scourge of mosquitoes. We had to leave the site, and then the whole night I slurped the luscious and sweetly fragrant wine.

In the morning, I had to finish leftover dishes from the previous night, and take a shower. I was stinking like a pig. I didn't want to give Garth any reason to question me for my condition. He sometimes bosses me around, although I am his boss. Maybe it's his care that makes him do that. He is already heartbroken after his wife's death, so I avoid quarreling with him frequently.

It's midnight and I just came back from the pharmacy. Not many customers are interested in our business anymore. Maybe diseases have dwindled, or they are just scared of me because what my last employee did, leaves no room for doubt that people are curious about my past. It was my fault that I trusted him and told him my secrets, but in return, he declared me mad. I think that boy was surrounded by many unrealistic series of events. He might have had some problem with his brain because nobody in his right mind cancels out the presence of a living person. Like I know he was just messing with me, but he left us in so much distress and mistrust that we had to take our time to explain everything to everyone. He just wanted to leave the job, and that's why he was making up these tales, pretty weird ones.

Drinking coffee and enjoying the sensuous feeling of the cold breeze make you feel as light as a feather. Recalling everything, and then giving words to my thoughts with my elephant tooth pen are the best parts of the day. As far as I remember, I and Stephen would sit and try to write different stuff in the diary. He used to go to school unlike me, so he would daily teach me the concepts he would learn there. However, I was home-schooled, taught by an intelligent mother, and supported by a brilliant father. Stephen's parents would admire our family for how happy and complete we were. Now, I see my childhood and my innocence in Willa. She is simply me.

When it's about to rain, a special aroma surrounds you, bewitching your mind by making you picture the wonders of nature. The rain clouds take charge of the sky, and the past of your present. I wish Willa could see it, but she is feeling unwell. Her hallucinations ruin everything. How can I put them to an end? It gets upsetting for me and painful for her. She is quite unfortunate, and so am I. Having a partner like Willa and not having her at the same time is something that kills me every day.

The roosters welcomed everyone to witness the marvels of the dawn. I didn't sleep at all. Willa had been resting in my arms the whole night, meanwhile, I kept caressing her hair and chasing the trails of the scent escaping her locks. This whole time, her gentle skin had been brushing mine, and her warmth had been radiating into my body. There couldn't be a better view to look up to while skipping sleep. Whenever she would look at me after abruptly waking in the middle of the night, I wouldn't be able to stop myself from weeping over her misery. I don't know how long this will continue.

She is looking stunning while sitting in that rocking chair, the one bearing its own set of memories in its wooden shafts. It was Dad's best friend during his last days. His paralyzed body would settle in this chair like a crumbling doll, and the chair would do its job quite well by keeping his fragile body from falling apart.

My house already smells like a stranded garden. Willa has a deep nostalgic connection with bonsai trees, so I bought her a few. Onerwaarten is a dry piece of land, and the farmers have to grow things like these in special green chambers. They add some more nutrients to it, making the moist smell even more noticeable. Mom used to love these too. Every Saturday, she would ask Dad to bring her a few. Stephen and I would take care of them, and our backyard was full of these, but it was only until I was 16. After that, I remember myself feeling quite shy while going back to Uncle Shane's shop all alone. It is 6 miles away from the pharmacy. These days, his son is carrying forward the legacy.

I bought some passion fruit and placed the packet on the counter near the guest room (which no one has opened for 10 years), and then went to the nearest internet cafe. I wanted to get done with an important piece of work. After getting done in an hour, I returned. The events following my return shook me to my core. The packet that I had left on the counter, was lying on the floor. It had been torn open, and the condition presented to me a gut-wrenching spectacle. It seemed as if the packet was discovered by a ferocious and hungry animal. The things didn't end there as the packet was stained with a few blood drops. The world sank before my eyes. It felt as if the floor wanted to suck me into it. I panicked and rushed towards my room. I kept screaming her name while searching for her everywhere.

"Willa!"

-No response-

2

28, November

A biker took a turn to Roueg Geheimnis Lane. He was looking for house no. 91. Finally, a colorful door caught his sight. He stopped there and left the flowers after giving a quick knock. Verrots's weather had welcomed ages ago a notorious component: humidity. In the area, there usually aren't any signs of wind at all. Everything seems lifeless. You can only see the gliding hawks ready to eat the flesh of your bones.

The environment was cunningly static that day, with no excitement at all. The land seemed to be inflicted by the worst drought as it looked completely barren, just a few lying rocks on a yellow bed cremating the dead plants. The trees here look haunted as if they are inhabited by witches. The fruits are usually rotten and surrounded by flies. Anyone who sees this land for the first time gets compelled to think that this land is cursed. There is a myth lingering in the towns that a battle took place on this barren land between the witches and some fairies. Fairies, the ones who are expected to be the loving ones, did something barbaric, thus narrating a wordless and bloody tale to the future generations. Their queen hanged many witches ruthlessly after triumphing in a brutal battle. The witches who managed to save themselves, invaded this city with a Satan-led cult to lead their revenge-driven story. Since then, everyone has been facing the repercussions led by those demonic chants, and no one has gotten to see the good days. The streams flowing here used to be crystal-clear, but now, the water has become unholy and filthy with the curse spells engraved on the wooden plaques settling deep down the water bodies. The sky once used to be home to the cotton woven throne, while the gardens would get infused with the colors concealing the bedazzling wonders of nature. The fruits grown before would bear extra sweetness in their flesh, but now, all the creatures in the surroundings are compelled to give up their sense of smell because of the rotting hue.

After hearing the knock, a woman in her late forties came out. She read the card placed on the flowers, it had 'From: Dwayne Steven' written on it. She was wearing a gray bed gown, hiding her face behind a veil to prevent the dust from settling on her face. Her body looked tanned to a perfect extent. Her eyes were cat-like, bewitchingly enticing. She picked up the bouquet, went in, and slammed the door angrily as if she was mad over something that had happened before she opened the door. She leaned forward to get a whiff of the appropriately scented flowers. The aroma made her skin blush as if all the pores in her face had blossomed. The unignorable trails of love-brewed scent took over her body with subtle excitement, and her worries ultimately surrendered.

Ulva is an Iranian. She has a noticeable aquiline nose, prominent cheekbones, and tattooed brows. She expects a jasmine bouquet after every night she has sex with Dwayne. They have to get shipped from a nearby city because of their exoticness. It is a tough call for Ulva to choose between jasmines and lilies, her new choices. She placed the flowers on the wooden rack next to her door. She went to the washroom and carried out her morning skincare routine, while Dwayne was still snoring in his striped night suit. After taking a shower, she went to the kitchen to prepare Dwayne and herself breakfast. To make herself stay content throughout the day, she prepared herself a cup of tea using cherry blossom extracts. The malodorous aroma filled the kitchen making her eyes squint with certain anticipation.

Half an hour later, Dwayne managed to leave the bed to get done with his morning rituals. Dwayne is two years older than Ulva. His deep blue eyes can make anybody fall for him. The spiraling folds in his iris hypnotize its exhibitors. The gray hair has never looked good on anybody except him. Although his physique looks fit, he lacks agility to a greater extent. In short, his body itself is an epitome of the marvels witnessed by many gerontologists, just like Ulva's. However, both of them bear contrasts to a greater extent in terms of intellect.

"Oh, so the bouquet is here," said Dwayne standing at some distance from the wooden rack.

"Yeah, it came in super early. I was sleepy so I didn't get to bewilder myself much with its smell." Ulva replied while swinging her arms to make an attempt at imitating the picturization of the aroma.

"I will go to bed again after you leave for work." She yawned while taking the bread slices out of the toaster.

"After passing the forties line, you have become dead-end lethargic." Dwayne chuckled.

There was silence for a moment and then he continued, "I smell fat, are you cooking the omelet in butter? I don't want to die the death of an obese."

"You forgot to bring olive oil yesterday. I had to get some butter from the neighbors. Now don't act like a fitness freak or I will shove this omelet down your throat."

"Ok, calm down. I will bring it after getting done with work."

"And don't forget to bring—" she stopped, "you know the drill, I feel passionless without them."

"You seriously need to work on your jokes, and as far as your request is concerned, sure." Dwayne winked.

Ulva prepared the table by plating everything delicately. After they were finished with breakfast, Dwayne went back to his room to get ready. Ulva turned her vacuum cleaner on and started cleaning her green Kazakhi mat with a tired gait. Her home is all color coordinated, seeking refuge in striking contrasts: yellow sofas with turquoise lamps. Even her bed matches this theme. She vacuumed the crippling leaves of the creeping ivies from the floor. The vines had been stifling the already suffocating cottage so Ulva tried to handle them accordingly.

Dwayne wore his mustard-colored shoes and was ready to leave for work.

"You look hot in this white shirt." Ulva smiled and moved forward to hand over Dwayne's tie, and then continued, "I can't remember who gave you this shirt. It looks expensive."

"What is so expensive about wearing a plain white shirt?" Dwayne's tone became stern as if something offended him.

His face perfectly showed the emptiness he felt inside after the resurfacing of some unappealing memory in his head. Ulva didn't notice his expressions. Instead, she waved her hand to ward him off while her eyes were stuck on her mobile screen. She seemed unbothered by the glances Dwayne passed. She tried to tackle the mystifying environment wittingly.

Dwayne entered a store smelling like Verbena, the famous French soap.

"Good morning mister." A boy bowed and greeted Dwayne.
"Good morning. Did we get any customers today?" asked Dwayne unenthusiastically while he rearranged the batteries on the counter.
"No, not a customer, but a man came to meet you."
"Did he tell you his name?"
"Yeah, a weird one. Plankton!"
Dwayne paused for a moment, gave a confused look, and then said, "Did he tell you anything else, like is he going to come again?"
"No sir, I mean he didn't tell me anything."
Dwayne took a deep breath. His heart began to beat fast against his chest, and his expressions turned into ones that perfectly depicted his hidden grievances. "Turn on the a.c, it's getting hot in here."

Something had started terrorizing Dwayne, as if

he was getting impacted by a heart-wrenching memory. He stumbled after a moment of distress, and started gasping for breath.

"Are you okay mister?" The boy looked concerned.
"Yeah, yeah. Just get me some water."
"Why is he here? What does he want?" Dwayne muttered.
"Here sir." Dwayne gulped down the water but he was still sweating profusely. Something was making him anxious.

At half past six, a stout man entered the shop. He was wearing tinted glasses, queer because the noon had already lost its hold, and the night had commenced a while ago. His face was half hidden by the khaki deerstalker. He was carrying a polished wooden staff. His trench coat seemed odd because it was warm outside. Anyone could tell from his looks that he was a traveler. His perfume was strong and non-native. His shoes were adding some more seriousness to his persona, while Dwayne could see the glares, reflecting from the shiny surface of the leather shoes, revealing his inner identity.

"Welcome! How may I help you?" asked Dwayne while cleaning a wine glass.
"Can I talk to Mr. Steven?" the man asked while looking at his watch.
"Yeah, it's me," replied Dwayne.

"Steven, it's Plankton." He removed his glasses, thus revealing his bulging eyes, and gazed at Dwayne cheerfully.

"Oh, oh— Plankton, you look so different. I didn't recognise you, really pleased to see you," he replied in a shaky voice.

Everything was true except the word *pleased.* Dwayne's expressions weren't settling well with his words. He had turned white from fear as if he just met a wanted serial killer.

"When did you become a detective? I remember you were a doctor." Dwayne laughed hysterically. Plankton passed a quirky smile and said, "Ah, I am still a doctor. This is my preferred attire for trips. I came here for the funeral of my dearest friend, and then I remembered that you live here so— How can someone like me forget you? You, me, and Erasmus—" Plankton paused as if he was being cautious with his words.

"It is great that you came here. Let's go to the nearest cafe, we can talk there in great detail."

"Great idea!" Plankton wore his shades and they both set off for the cafe.

The moon was brighter than ever. The sky was all clear. By then, a cool breeze had started resurrecting every lifeless thing. Dwayne and Plankton walked in silence. The awkwardness at that moment was a mystery in itself. The sound of footsteps was echoing in the street as if both of them were heavy with their thoughts. Finally, they arrived at the cafe. The cafe was empty, and the condition indicated that it had remained like this for quite some time.

"Umm— So where were we?" Dwayne looked lost. After much thought, he continued, "How did you get my address?" Dwayne tried to dissipate the constant awkwardness which was accompanying them for the last 20 minutes.

Their relation looked complicated, even though a showy frankness had reunited them at the store. Maybe they were pretending it in front of the boy there.

"Back in Onerwaarten, you told me about your plans. You were thinking of moving to Verrot. You also told me about your possible shifting to Roueg Geheinmnis Lane, so I decided to visit you. Though you don't seem happy over this reunion."

"Obviously I am happy— Don't worry! So tell me, how is everything back there?— like our street? — the people?" Dwayne took long pauses while asking this. He looked stunned for no reason.

"Everything is perfectly fine back there. If you are asking about Vernon, I haven't visited him since Erasmus' death. That poor boy has suffered a lot, but he is a strong boy," said Plankton in a secretive and cautious tone.

"Look! If you are here to make me feel bad, then

you can leave now. I just don't feel like looking back at all." By now, Dwayne's face had started showing the rage that was taking over his body.

"No, I swear, I swear I wanted to meet you! As we all used to be great friends. I wanted to see your face again."

"I am not remorseful for anything. Ulva and I are happy, and we want to stay happy."

"It's good, I mean great, but as I have already told you, making you guilty is none of my plans. We can't undo what's already—" Dwayne interrupted Plankton, "My life is already miserable. I don't want to talk to you anymore, and it's better if we forget our dreadful past because it was a dirty game played by destiny. It was nice meeting you. You may leave now."

"I was here just to meet you. As I am done with it, I was already thinking of leaving."

Plankton left his chair. He felt heartbroken and looked upset after the fiery exchange that had spurred abruptly between them. He tossed his staff and left the cafe by giving a fierce push to the door. Dwayne kept sitting in his chair like a terrorized cat; he had started shivering. His body had begun to slowly bend inwards. He tried to tuck his head between his legs. He attempted to stand up two times but stumbled and fell back. He was getting a panic attack. After a few minutes, he calmed down and set off for his store once again.

Around midnight, he came back to his house in a wrecked condition. He was holding his files in one hand and in the other, a plastic bag that had a bottle of olive oil and 1kg of passion fruit. He removed his shoes, went in, and placed the things on the counter. Wilting Jasmine flowers caught his attention. He sprinkled some water on them, but all to no avail. He opened the windows to see the bright moon but the squeaky sound of rusting metal was all that he could get. For a moment, he impulsively attempted to catch the strings of his losing breath while thinking about something terrifying. Then he called Ulva. She didn't respond. Dwayne was very hungry; he wanted Ulva to cook him something. He went to his room to see whether Ulva was there, but she wasn't. Then he went to the living room. Ulva was sleeping on the couch in front of the muted TV. Dwayne intended to wake her up but it was already midnight. He changed his clothes and slept next to Ulva with his head on the couch, while his lower body was leaning against her.

"I love you," Dwayne mumbled, and then closed his eyes.

3

The sight was as if someone could picture the scene of her death. Willa was lying on the floor. Blood was smeared on the walls as if she had tried to hold something to walk properly. When I went near her, she was still breathing, but at that moment her eyes were telling me that she wanted to die. She was in great pain. I wore my shoes, rushed to Mr. Plankton's house, although a psychiatrist could do nothing, I was in need of a helping hand. I thought he was the only one who could have a professional say in this. Just before ringing his bell, I realized that it had already been three years since he left our street. When I returned, Willa had started turning blue. I then decided to call the ambulance.

"Hello, here I have a medical emergency," I said the second someone picked up my call. I was shivering and that shiver was eventually replaced by a fierce tremor.

"Hey, we are listening to you. How can we help you?" a woman spoke.

"My wife is vomiting blood. I think she ate something poisonous. Please send someone as early as possible."

"Ok, we are sending an ambulance. Please tell me your address."

After 10 minutes, an ambulance reached my door. The paramedics entered my house. There were two men and one woman. I showed them the way to the room where I had left Willa. To everyone's surprise, when we entered the room, she wasn't there. They started staring at me with annoyed gazes as if I had lied.

"She was lying here. Let me check the washroom."

I checked the washroom, she wasn't even there. The fact that severely shocked me was that the blood smears too had disappeared. I was completely lost.

"Please tell us where the patient is! We can't see anybody here. You know that you can face serious charges if you have called us for no reason."

"No, trust me, she was here! I was with her a few moments before you arrived."

"Stop wasting our time. Legal proceedings will be carried out against you if you keep lying to

us."
"How can I make you trust me? She was here! Please don't call the cops."
"Check the house once again," said one of them.

I was almost crying and I searched the whole house again. Now, there were two things bothering me; firstly, where did Willa go, and secondly, these people were going to send me to jail just because of an illusion that led to confusion. Even after searching for her for fifteen minutes, I couldn't find her.

"I am extremely sorry. I can't understand what is happening."
"David, check the house for the final time," said the lady in them.

After a few minutes, he came back with a disappointed and frustrated face.

"Mam, there is no one except him in the house. I didn't even find anything hinting at the presence of a woman."
"A lot of time has been wasted already. We hope this is just a misunderstanding. We are leaving you this time, but beware of doing this again! Otherwise, you will have to pay a hefty amount as a fine, and you can even go to jail." After giving me this warning, they all left the house.

I fell to my knees. I was feeling miserable about

what just happened. Tears were rolling down my cheeks. My head was about to burst, and my heart was about to leave my chest. I seemed like a complete psychopath at that time. Words can't describe the extreme confusion that I felt, and the way it left me bewildered. I had to live a few moments of aggravating devastation.

Even after one week, I can't fully digest the way events have unfolded before my eyes. Willa's simple move could have proven disastrous for me, but after all, it was a misunderstanding. I still want to ask her why she went to that guest room at a time when an ambulance was there to take her to the hospital. There are a lot of questions in my mind. And how did I miss that guest room while searching for her? Maybe because no one had ever entered that room for years. I found her after an hour of searching, while I had almost started gasping for air. The thing that boggled me the most was that her condition looked different from the one in which I had left her. When I found her, she looked alright.

The guest room was opened after ten years. Last time, Dad's best friend stayed in it. That was after he and his wife separated. He and Dad had a strange friendship, sometimes unexplainable. They had a partnership in a business venture. He was heartbroken after his separation, and that's why he decided to leave Onerwaarten. Who knew, the friendship of years would come to such an abrupt end. He never came back. Then after that, no one bothered to open the guest room.

The guest room has a huge queen-size bed. We would only use silk bed sheets, as Mom had a belief that hospitality should never be compromised. I suggested to her those wooden lamps resting on the wrecked side tables. We bought them from a small shop which was managed by an elderly Chinese woman. It was the most ancient and uniquely crafted piece out of all the pieces available there, so we picked it. Going to that room after such a long time led to a heart-aching reminiscence of memories, which drove me to a verge where I broke into tears. How Dad and I used to play hide and seek in there, was a separate memory to make me sob. The marble cupboard, the perfect hiding spot, presented its own set of memories. Now, the whole room is infested by insects. The golden threads with which the sheets were once sewn, have already withered, thus sewing a new ugly piece symbolizing the current darkening times. The wooden floor is almost eaten by termites. I couldn't stay in that room for more than a few minutes without losing my sanity because of the following reasons: firstly, this room is a heart-wrenching monument for a series of events, the ones that I don't want to relive. Everyone is gone so it is of no use to get stuck in the self-sucking pit of traumatic memories. Secondly, if these things wouldn't make me whimper terrifically, the dust was enough to fill my sputum with blood and bring back my long-lost allergies.

I grabbed my childhood favorite book: "To kill a Mockingbird" from the stand rusting in one corner of the room, and left the place. Mom would narrate this book to me before going to bed, and now, I wanted to relive those moments with Willa. Her condition isn't well, and her sickness can't leave her alone for even the faintest moment. The spells cast on her don't seem to be losing their hold any time soon. I can't even talk to her properly as she gets tremors. I have a lot of questions to ask from that day, but her health deprives me of all such opportunities. I can't lose her; she is the only reason for me to live.

I made her lie down on the bed and read her the book. She kept gazing at the ceiling, and then eventually closed her eyes. I placed the book on the side table and went for a walk. The weather was breezy. I wanted my existence to dissolve in the serene surroundings. It felt as if the gentle strokes from nature, impacting my body, were healing my wounds: the wounds that couldn't be seen, but were infesting my heart and disturbing my intellect. However, there is also a reason to hate this weather as one cloudy day announced the death of my dad, but then I will have to hate a portion of my life, the portion that doesn't deserve this treatment at least, so this finally becomes a matter of dilemma for me.

The morning Dad died was a usual one. I was preparing breakfast. Dad would love a toast with peanut butter applied to it. I was scooping out some peanut butter when I suddenly heard a thud as if someone fell. I rushed towards Dad's room. He was lying on the floor, while his head was stuck between the tires of the wheelchair, and the look in his eyes delivered me the message that all the signs of life were already closing their doors for him. He was dead by the time I found him. Later, it was revealed that he died due to myocardial infarction caused by a thrombus formed in his leg. That day was one of the days when I felt that I was always meant to be abandoned. I thought there was no one left to take care of me, there was no one left to stop me from throwing tantrums on unexpected occasions, there was no one left to make me laugh, and that day was the day that stretched its horizons taking the rest of my life in its wrath. That day I fell apart forever, and I had already realized that there was no going back. I can't eat anything on the day I recall this darkening memory. The reminiscence can't get any easier for me even if a few years have passed.

Dad and I had a unique bond. Those Thursday walks can never be forgotten. Dad was the Santa

Claus for all of my wishes, from buying me my favorite books to taking me on trips, there is a long list that I owe him for. He never made me leave his cloak of care and supervision. Whenever I would do my homework, he would bring me chocolates and gummies, and then at night, he would get me ice cream. Brushing with him at night was something that I would daily look up to. Even after getting minor injuries, the panic in his eyes would give me a sensation that he could never see me in pain.

Dad took my full responsibility. He tried his best to take care of an autistic son like me. I used to be a bit oversensitive, but he still provided me with every facility to put me at ease. He homeschooled me. He was a magnificent throne-like cloud that would take every person in its shade of mercy.

His best friend, who would share a fatherly bond with me, handed over his pharmacy to Dad before leaving Onerwaarten. The business saw its peak with Dad. From working diligently, to being fair and honest, everything accounted for the pharmacy's success. Furthermore, may Lord bless him for what he would do for orphans. Garth came to us at a young age, his uncle brought him. My dad taught him the work at the pharmacy, and sent him to a prestigious institution for his studies. He never discriminated between us too. Once, some boys teased Garth for being an orphan, but Dad went to their homes and made them apologize for their mischievous act, and made them realize the fact that Garth was no longer alone. This incident has always stayed with me.

Dad fell from the stairs at the age of 34. This was what stole from him his livelihood. He sort of lost the true essence of his life. I wasn't present there but Mom told me that Lucy, our cat, made Dad trip over. It caused permanent paralysis of his lower body. I didn't see him smile often after that day. The night before his death, he was asking me to gird up loins for the difficult times that had to come. He foretold me about the emotionally straining phase of my life that was soon going to poison my existence. He told me that it was very important for me to deal with it maturely, otherwise, I could stumble. I don't know whether I dealt with the circumstances well, but without any doubt, Willa helped me in every way by dividing the burden. The day when his final rites were being carried out, I realized that I wasn't all alone. Even though I couldn't physically find anybody around, but mentally, I never felt the need for a companion. I don't know how, but there always has been someone sharing with me my space in my thoughts. I have this strange feeling all the time that Dad is watching me from heaven. Maybe he sent Willa as his replacement. After his death, I joined his pharmacy with Garth, and this is where I am now. I want to create a similar impact as he did.

Willa's stomach was swollen this morning. She is suffering from excruciating aches with constipation. She woke up with a dry mouth, and even some heartburn. I have already read about this, these are all the side effects of her medications. She is terrified by the recurring hallucinations. She can't even sleep peacefully for a few minutes. She explained everything to me, like what she had been seeing. A man in his twenties, with hazel eyes and ginger-colored hair, chases her every time. She tries to hide from him but he follows her with the intention to seek revenge. That man is everywhere. She said that she could see him as a black shadow escaping the vents of the room. This all sounds strange but this is what schizophrenia does to a person. Everything becomes an illusion.

I had some lychees in my fridge. I blended it with soda and gave it to Willa for her heartburn. I know this isn't a medical solution, but she must be tired of her medication. I made her go on a walk with me, it helps her frequently. At home, I left some broccoli boiling as it's good for constipation.

There weren't any wind sounds, just the noise of a few kids playing in the next street. It was refreshing to see the restoration of the liveliness in our street too. However, strange things are always there to scare off your happy moments, and the evil eye hunted us down here too. I and Willa were walking peacefully when a few children came from the next street and started laughing at me for no reason. It made me uncomfortable. They were triggering my autistic behavior, but I tried to stay composed for Willa. We returned to our home within a few minutes. It was difficult for me to stop thinking about it the whole night.

In the morning, I decided to update my photo album. I made Willa sit in Dad's chair and took some photos on my phone, as I thought that it would be great to take photos of two of the closest things to my heart from the present, Dad's chair and Willa. After taking a printout of those photos, I am going to add them to my collection.

4

THE FIRST SYMBOL

5, December

Ulva was listening to a podcast while lying on her couch. Suddenly, she heard a revolting thunder. There was excitement on her face for the weather, but soon, a reminder of some fear started making her feel dizzy. This kind of fear clings to her intellect whenever nature presents a nightmarish scene, however, this time she made an attempt to not let this fear influence the rush of excitement in her body. To showcase her happiness, she screamed joyfully. She did everything to prevent the blackish hue from settling on her present.

It began to drizzle. Everything started smelling fresh as it rained after a long dry spell. Ulva sniffed the moist mud in her hands which she scooped out of the plant pot. She spread her arms and started twirling in the rain. The mud dissolved in rainwater kept flowing down the folds of the wrinkles on her body, moistening all the pores in its way. The sensuous feeling of rainwater running down her thighs kept arousing her. By now, she was already looking forward to the steamy sex she was going to have that night.

Ulva made herself a cup of tea and sat on the soft couch while letting the weather do its magic on her. She tried to compose a tune orchestrated by the raindrops sliding against the wide window panes of her house. She ended up with a melancholic song seeping through the convolutions of her brain while triggering some specific emotions. When she dissected the song, she was left with bits that described her traumatic past.

After finishing her tea, she went outside for some time. She unclipped her hair and started twirling again. She enjoyed the rain to her fullest, but it didn't last long because the rain started revealing its true intention: the intention to write a gut-wrenching story down the history. She returned to her home but nothing seemed to stop her from relishing inside too. The raindrops from the long-awaited shower kept hitting the roof of her house, making the whole house echo with their sound. After that, a dreamy sequence started to unravel before her eyes as if the thunder had started resonating with the thunder in her life. After one hour, the gentleness of the showers was completely overtaken by the ferociousness of the hail; while on the other hand, a cunning sadness had started to overpower Ulva's unaffected relish. It might have been her fears from the past casting such spells on her. The constant reminder of some ugly truth kept dragging her to a state of restlessness, right after the moments she spent rejoicing. The memory of one of her loved ones dying in such weather got her teary-eyed. The storm made her relive all the upsetting memories of her life clinging to this basic phenomenon. The knots this thread of memories was bearing, somehow made her sulk from certain regrets that were breeding her upsetting past.

While she was lost somewhere in her guilt trip, a black cat jumped onto her balcony. This freaked her out and a mere jumpscare made her start panting. When she was assured by all the happenings of the day that this weather wasn't working for her, she went for a quick shower to rinse her hair, and decided to get back to listening to the podcast.

She was blow-drying her hair when she heard someone knocking at her door. It was a loud knock. Ulva expected it to be Dwayne outside, but he would have used the key. She leapt to open the door out of curiosity, but what she saw after opening it, made shivers run down her spine. An old injured woman was shivering vehemently from the cold. Her body looked as if it was going to crumble into dust, and then get washed away by the rain. Her clothes were completely drenched. Her scarf had soaked in so much water that her neck was bending downwards due to the weight. Her legs were muddy up to her knees, and her almost bald head had bruises. Her big bulgy eyes looked sleep deprived and it seemed as if she had been crying for quite a long time. She was squinting because of the lack of energy to keep her eyes wide open. Ulva without any hesitation took her inside. The woman, in her late 60s, was struggling with the heavy knotted sack on her back. Ulva helped her with it.

Ulva took out a black velvet dress from her closet for that woman. The clothes in her sack were all torn and old. They were thin and she could catch a cold in them. Ulva held her by her shoulders and took her to the bathroom. She prepared the bathing tub for her by filling it with hot water. The woman was too fragile to bathe herself so Ulva bathed her instead. Her eyes were instantly filled with gratitude and they kept giving Ulva a sensation that she was praying for her.

> "I will pray to God to keep all the worries a thousand miles away from you. I wish I could have a child like you," the woman said with her

quivering voice.
"Dear lady, your prayers mean a lot."
"Do you have any kids?" the woman asked with great concern.

Ulva looked confused as if some old pain hit her again. Her expressions further showed that a bundle of regrets had started pressing her intellect. She mustered up her courage to reply,

"No, I wish I had." Tears rolled down her cheeks.
"It's ok, or even completely fine. At least you don't have any fear of getting hurt by them."
Ulva stayed silent till she was done bathing that lady.
"Wear these clothes and get warm. I am going to prepare some food for you." Ulva handed over the clothes that she had chosen for her.
"Thank you!" the woman said softly and quietly.

Ulva got the table ready. She made that woman sit comfortably at the dinner table.

"Here is some corn soup, boiled rice with peas, broccoli, and some salad. What would you like to take first?"
"I think I have forgotten how to eat. I can't even remember how these things taste."

Ulva looked sorry for her. She made her eat some rice and salad. It was a hard task because the old woman seemed discontented with everything going on around her. The look on her face explained that she was trying to avoid a confrontation with some traumatic memory triggered by her surroundings. Ulva tried her best to calm her down. After the dinner was over, Ulva made herself and that lady some tea.

"What's your name? I forgot to ask you earlier," Ulva tried to restart the conversation.
"Samantha, the unlucky Samantha. That's what everyone used to call me."
"Unlucky, what made you unlucky? I mean you are such a charming woman."
"I used to be charming, just like you. But I don't know what made me so unmotherly. I was known for my family, but I don't know what made me ignore such a great blessing from God. A mother is known to be so angelic, but I let Satan influence my moves in many ways. It is all my fault, all my—" Samantha's eyes had started twitching as if they had run out of tears, or as if she had forgotten the ways to grieve over her pains.
"I never experienced motherhood but mothers in my life have played an essential role. After my dad left us, Mom proved herself to be the man of the house. Mother is without any doubt an angel. She would wipe our tears when nobody wanted to lend us their sleeve. She tried her best to make our sob turn into giggles." Ulva started pouring out her heart after listening to Samantha.

"But after all, she is a human too! Every human is flawed, she can be too. But this doesn't give her a reason to be selfish. I was selfish! Do you know why I am not crying over my luck? It's because there is nothing unexpected happening to me. I am reaping what I sowed," said Samantha mournfully.

"I don't want to ask you this but what so significant happened to make you think this way?" Ulva asked out of curiosity.

"It's a long story, so long that I won't be able to complete it in my lifetime, but I have a question for you. Did your father ever look back? Did he ever try to come back to you and get everything sorted?"

"No, he didn't. Even if he would ever try to do so, there was no way we were going to accept him back. It isn't just because of what he did to us, but in actuality, he had insulted the institution of fatherhood. He doesn't deserve to get forgiven," Ulva said with all her might. She uttered these words so quickly that she didn't even realize what she said. Realizing after a few seconds, she looked lost as if what she had said was somehow canceling her whole existence.

"Just replace your dad with me, your family with mine and my story is explained. Today, I just went back as if I was still his mother, but after reaching there, I discovered my true self and position by just looking into his sorrowful eyes. I didn't even have the right to ask him for forgiveness. The strange thing is that even today I went for a selfish reason. I thought of it as an opportunity, an opportunity to get care and love for the rest of my life because of the simple fact that I have given birth to him. I went there for my gain. My greed didn't go away even in such circumstances. The push to my son, which was supposed to be a goodbye when I left him, came all the way back to me. I pushed him for all the wrong reasons but he pushed me for his own good. That's why I can't complain."

She continued after taking a deep breath, "I felt connected to him in the truest of meanings after getting neglected by him like this. But who cares what I feel? It was me who made him suffer and I am the one to be punished. He seemed to be doing just fine when I met him today, but only he knows what he has gone through. There is quite a possibility that his apparent well-being was just an illusion." Samantha looked relieved after opening up and confessing everything.

Her cough distracted Ulva as she was lost in her thoughts once again.

"Let me get you cough syrup," she said.
As Ulva tried to stand up, Samantha held her hand and said, "Let me die, I have lived more than I deserve."
"You are burning hot, you have a fever. Oh my God, let me get you something immediately."

Ulva rushed to the storeroom and got her hands on some medicines for cough and pyrexia.

> "Take these!" She kneeled close to Samntha's chair and extended her arm to hand over the medicine. Samantha refused to take them by gently nodding her head left and right.
> "Please take them, dear lady. You have to live for yourself."
> "Can I stay here till tomorrow morning?"
> "By all means! I wasn't going to let you leave anyway. Let me get the room ready for you."

Ulva went to the guest room, removed the old and dusty bed sheet, and replaced it with a new one. She led Samantha to the room. The room had a royal setting. The olive green bed sheet kept revealing the shimmering threads tracing the edges of the bed. The antique lamps were making the room look grandeur. The beautiful Jasmine aroma and a strong musk made the place feel heavenly.

> "I don't deserve it but thank you for this hospitality." Samantha tried to gesture with her wrecked body but she was too weak to move on her own.
> "Mention not, you are a beautiful human. Nothing makes your dignity less! Good night."
> "May you stay happy forever," murmured Samantha.

Ulva left the room to eat some painkillers for her migraine, she looked distressed. The rain had stopped. She opened the windows to let in some fresh air. The moment she opened them, the aroma of the moist mud instantly diffused into every corner of the house. She tried to fall asleep after taking medicine but some thoughts kept making her uneasy. She tried to wait for Dwayne too but he didn't come back till midnight.

6, December

In the morning, Ulva woke up before everyone. She found Dwayne by her side. She smiled and got ready to prepare breakfast. She went to the guest room to check on Samantha but she was still fast asleep. Ulva decided not to disturb her and went back to get done with the chores.

After everyone was done with breakfast, Ulva decided to check on Samantha once again as she had shown no signs of waking up before too, and it had been more than 15 hours since Ulva left her in the room. She went to wake her up but the sight that she looked at was not appealing at all. Samantha's fragile body was turning pale in the bed. Ulva looked concerned about her condition so she gently tapped on her face. Samantha didn't respond. Ulva repeated the act but there was still no response, so she panicked. She checked her pulse but there were no signs of her being alive. Ulva impulsively dialed the emergency number. After a brief examination by the paramedics, Samantha was declared dead.

"She died a few hours ago," said the lady nurse.

Out of courtesy, Ulva and Dwayne fulfilled Samantha's final rites. At the graveyard, many strangers had gathered to say a final goodbye to her.

"Poor lady. She never got to see happiness in her life," said a woman in them.
"Do you know her?" Ulva inquired.
"Yes, she lived at the end of our street. She lived with her adopted son. The day he found out about his adoption, happiness didn't see the way to this poor lady's house."

Everyone started leaving the graveyard after getting done with the rites and Ulva walked out with that woman.

"Why did she adopt him? I mean I am not at a place to ask this but—" asked Ulva.
"After multiple miscarriages with her second husband, she had to take this step. But still, this poor soul tried her best to take care of that boy. She and her husband gave that boy the best education, and provided him with all the basic necessities. They loved him more than anything

in this world"

"Then what happened to her? Like why was she thrown out of her house?"

"Her son found out about his adoption a few years ago but his financial needs wouldn't let him do anything, after all, that house was Samantha's property. Unfortunately, a few months back her husband died and her son, whom we all call a *heartless monster* now, threw her out of her own house."

"Oh, Oh—" Ulva looked stunned.

"But she told me something else," Ulva mumbled.

"What did she tell you?" the woman asked.

"She said that she had abandoned her son and now karma was hitting back at her."

"She must have told you about her first marriage. She spent most of the days of her life in constant regret as far as we know. By the way, we hadn't heard from her for quite a while. We didn't know that she was thrown out of her house until today."

"We should have called her son," said Ulva.

"I asked my husband to give him the news but he ignored the call. He is rightly called *a heartless monster*."

Ulva was devastated after burying Samantha. She kept thinking about her on the way back to her home. The conversation she had with her kept playing on repeat in her head.

5

Nothing normal happened in the last few weeks. One might say that they were stressful, but for me, surviving them was equally emotionally challenging. Police have already made 5 rounds to investigate the accident that happened at the pharmacy. Whatever happened, it disgusted everyone to their cores and must have left them with some deep-rooted fear. Even my detective radar is now on and I want to find out Garth's ruthless murderer. I always heard that crimes happen in the darkest streets but in this case, somebody robbed a grown man of breath in broad daylight. The murderer has to be someone with a maligned conscience and merciless heart because the footage from the crime scene presented an utterly heartbreaking spectacle.

It was a normal morning and I was all set to attend my pharmacy. The time was around nine in the morning. When I opened the pharmacy door, the unexpected and heart-wrenching sight made my body stiff and my breath shallow. Garth was lying on the floor with a gruesome cut on his head. Some gel-like substance was oozing out and the wounds looked swollen. His body looked empty as if all the blood had gushed out. His eyes were wide open and there were some tears frozen in the stunned domes of his pupil. His eyes had captured a look as if they had been in quest of someone before the expiration of the body. The dried tears forming crusty stains on his cheeks hinted at him losing the courage to find a helping hand. I can't explain the pain I felt at that moment. I have been mumbling this very question since discovering his body in the pharmacy, "Why couldn't I save him?"

On further look, I saw things that shattered me completely. Garth's eyes were half-filled with blood. A sharp object had inflicted his head as we found a serrated knife stuck in his skull. Near him, we found a metal rod which explained the origin of multiple bruises on his body, a big bottle of glycerine spilled all over the floor mixed with his lumpy blood, and a shattered pane of glass piercing his right thigh, while the flesh could be seen to have gotten detached from the bone. I can still recall the moment I impulsively took him in my arms after seeing his destitute body. My nervous voice echoed in the empty pharmacy while calling an ambulance, and the shallow breaths were numbing my body. That final goodbye to him, when the paramedics were taking him away, is going to be written as one of the hardest ones in the history of friendships. Another friendship of two decades ended tragically.

Asking his kids for patience while knowing that Garth was never going to come back, needed a portion of me having the appropriate amount of determination. The police made multiple rounds to ask the people about the glimpses of the scene they had caught. They interrogated me too. They are hopeful that they will solve the mystery, though the mystery doesn't look easy.

> "Was he enemies with someone dangerous?" asked one of the officers.
> "I don't know much but I saw him being upset for the past few months. He would quarrel with someone on the phone. I didn't dare to ask him," I answered.
> "Can you give us a few names? Those whom you find suspicious? As you told us that you were close to him, so you might know the people he was surrounded by."
> "Officer, as I told you, we never got to discuss these things. Even the disturbing calls don't date back quite far. He was a peace-loving guy and would always avoid conflicts." I answered abruptly.
> "Ok, we will further investigate this matter and see if the evidence covers something that can

help us. We will also talk to his children if needed."

The officer was about to leave the room when I said, "Officer! I have a request. Please don't involve those innocent kids. They have already been left distraught after the death of both of their parents. We don't know what they must be going through. We shouldn't disturb them until they decide to speak up themselves."

"Ok, we'll see," said the officer while half turned, and then he left the pharmacy.

It was now necessary to visit Garth's kids. This cruel world was almost too much for them to tolerate. Their young innocent minds couldn't comprehend these complexities. When I visited them, they were packing their stuff. Their aunt Shayna had arrived. She revealed her plans to adopt the kids.

"I came here once before too to take these kids when Mariya died, but they wanted to stay with their dad. Now, there is no way I would leave them here alone. They are my sister's living memory," she said.

"That's a good idea. Take them away as early as possible. They need some rest: emotionally, mentally, and physically. I don't want them to get exhausted with these officers coming in daily and then interrogating them."

"Don't worry. Everything has been planned already. I will adopt them if something like this becomes a need."

Then after saying a final goodbye to them, I came back home with a heavy heart. Everything has burnt into ashes within a glimpse. I don't know when I will get to see them again, and I feel helpless too as I can't bring my dear friend back.

Garth was brought to my father at a young age. He used to dream big. He belonged to a poor family while his father had already died. They would sleep hungry most nights. Garth wanted to earn a better living for the remaining members of his family. My father wholeheartedly welcomed him and hired him as a cashier. He eventually proved himself to be of great use to him. It didn't take him long to become a beloved individual in our family. I can't forget those weekends I would spend with him in the winter. I still have his coffee mug with me in my cupboard. We would take sips from our 'Brothers Forever' mugs while trying to act tipsy after drinking strongly brewed coffee. Then Dad would tell us about his dreamy childhood and our brains would get clouded with different thoughts.

My dad married Garth to a bread seller's daughter. Garth loved her and wanted to marry her. Dad took his proposal to her house and then the drama which stirred up that day, became another unforgettable memory to laugh at. They didn't accept the proposal at first, but a few days later, they agreed to marry their daughter to Garth.

My relationship with him became much stronger after Dad's death. He tried his best to console me. He managed the pharmacy without me for quite some time. He and Willa were my only support system. He outdid himself by always being there for me in the darker times. But Garth too saw his lows as he lost his liveliness after his wife's death. She was diagnosed with breast cancer and Garth didn't have money for her treatment. But the behavior that inspired me the most was the way he made the odds work for him. He didn't let such an unexpected hiccup affect his life adversely and tried to think practically instead. He had to live for his kids and he did. Alas, I am just left with his memories now.

I went outside for a walk to distract myself from these suffocating thoughts, and to breathe some air with the hope of finding some dispersed particles of ecstasy in it. The clouds had already formed a fluffy blanket in the sky, while I got grossly engaged with the hungry cat circling me. I was buying myself a loaf of fresh bread when a man in his late sixties showed up and came up to me.

"Vernon, Is it you?"

"Yeah, do you know me?" I replied confidently.

The man was wearing well-ironed clothes, and the maroon color was complimenting his fair complexion. He looked older than his age; I assumed it from his gait. He had a well-trimmed white beard. He was squinting through his thin-frame glasses. His shoes were super clean as if they had some inbuilt mechanism to clean off the dirt on them, as there was not even a single speck of dust to be seen. He was making the air get even more suffocating with his strongly-scented perfume.

"Oh my boy, it's a pleasure to see you after so long. You have grown into a handsome man."
"Thank you, but may I ask you who you are?"
"I am Plankton. Your neighbor and your father's friend. Did you forget me?"
"Oh, oh, didn't recognize you at all. This beard and style were never there. I am really pleased to see you."
"I just can't stop looking at you. I am really happy that you dealt with things like this. After all, you are the son of a man whose maturity would always make us feel lucky for having him as a friend."
"I won't be giving much credit to myself as this magic has been done on me by the love of my life, Willa. God gave me a perfect gift so I didn't have any right to displease Him by torturing myself

for long."

"Oh wow, so you are married? I mean of course because I saw the ring but, Umm—Congratulations! Erasmus would be so happy to see you well settled. I would love to meet that lucky lady."

"Please visit us someday. She is the true embodiment of mom. She is my everything, a friend, a motherly figure, and a lover."

"Now I see where these sweet words are coming from." He smiled cheerfully.

After a short period of silence, I continued, "Recently, time could have gotten a bit easier on me and Willa, but unfortunate events can't stop happening and we can't stop worrying." I sighed from sadness as Garth's death scene flashed across my mind once again.

Both of us started walking slowly.

"Good to know that you are doing fine, in fact, I am more than happy for you." Mr.Plankton patted my back.

"We are just talking about me but tell me about yourself! How are you? Like where have you been? Last time, if I recall, I saw you at Dad's funeral."

"Yeah, I got a call letter from a prestigious university for the professorship. As I was not doing well at my clinic, I decided to give it a go."

"I remember you were doing fine, like at least earning enough to light your stove. What more does a bachelor need?"

"You can say it was my greed more than my needs that made me leave this wonderful street." He hesitatingly chuckled.

"So are you back forever?"

"For now, things seem like this."

"Ah— That's great!"

"I am reopening my clinic. Like the people might still know me, although it has been a while since I practiced last time."

"They will be lucky to get your services once again."

"I don't think they would remember me with pleasant stuff. Anyways, what are you up to these days?"

"I am still working at Dad's pharmacy, although it got completely vandalized a few days ago. Someone broke in and attacked Garth. Unfortunately, that poor soul couldn't make it."

"Oh my Lord, mercy! How is his family doing?"

"His wife passed away a few years ago, while his kids just moved out with their aunt."

"Oh, may Lord bless his soul. It is heartbreaking news."

"Yeah, the police are still investigating the case."

"Those monstrous figures should taste the bitter fruit of justice."

"I hope they do! You seem tired, I think you should get some rest. Come to my house, you will get a good rest there."

"Yeah, I am planning to visit soon but not now," he paused for a few seconds, and then continued, "the time has changed a lot, or maybe it's us who have changed. Look, now we have phones to make things easy for us. A few years back, there was nothing besides a landline, and that too would hardly connect us to the riches of the city."

"I don't know what we should call ourselves now. The fortunate ones, or the most unfortunate. I am sorry, I am making you talk so much. You should probably get some rest."

"No, it's ok. It was just a journey, not a big deal. It is incomparable to the happiness I am feeling after seeing you. By the way, I am coming from Verrot. I went there to attend the funeral of a dear colleague."

I had no words to respond to this. I don't know why my tongue couldn't utter any word. I tried to say something, but my mouth couldn't make enough sound to make him hear. He continued talking without noticing my anxiety.

"There, I met our old friend Dwayne. He is still very passionate about his work, and works at a store." Mr.Plankton tried to counter the sudden awkwardness that struck us for a moment.

"Oh, I think I have heard this name before too, but can't remember the person. Can you tell me a

bit more?" My voice was breaking by now.
"He was a dear friend of your dad. He worked with him at the pharmacy. You were too young when he left for Verrot."
"Ok— Now I remember. So how is he?"
"He is good, doing well at his job, I mean at his store. He is living a happy married life. Although our first meeting wasn't an ideal one, I will try to get back to him soon."
I didn't say anything in response because my heart was racing, so he continued instead, "We had a brief session of talk. He still remembers you—," He stopped here and immediately held me by my shoulders.
"Is everything ok? You are breathing heavily."

I don't know why I started breathing heavily. My chest was wheezing, my hands were trembling, and my heart kept sinking. My eyes had started to fill with tears. I was getting a panic attack. After getting hold of myself, I made an attempt to say something,

> "No, I am ok! Just have these panic attacks sometimes, or it can be those typical asthma attacks."

Mr.Plankton took some medicine out of his bag, placed the pills under my tongue, and gave me water. Within a few minutes, I started to feel normal again.

"It is ok, we can talk later. I will be staying at my house for the major portion of the day. If you need any sort of help, I will be there."

"You must be tired too. Willa and I will be waiting for you. Please pay a visit soon."

"Sure, sure, I will. Take care!"

I bid him farewell and headed back to my house. In the middle of my detour, he called me by my name and I stopped. I turned back to listen to what he had to say.

"Yes mister, want to say something?" I asked.

He took some folded paper out of his pocket and handed it to me. "This fell from your pocket in the graveyard on Dwayne's funeral, never opened it but kept it safe. I tried to return it before going too but your condition wouldn't allow me."

I took the paper and thanked him. I started walking towards my home again. On my way, I stopped for a few moments to watch the innocent souls play in our street. That whole night, I kept thinking about my unexpected reunion with Mr. Plankton. I had somehow seen a glimpse of my dad in him, and this was granting me some peace.

6

THE THIRD SYMBOL

19, December

The roads were empty and seemed endless. Some mysterious smell was lingering in the air. The clouds had descended as if they were there to take someone with them to the heavens. The night was not a regular one; it was entangled in the most unexplainable emotions. The trees had lowered their branches in respect. The only sound that echoed in the streets was some heavy footsteps. A man with a strange gait was gripping the streetlights to keep his walk steady. He looked exhausted as if he was drained of even the last bit of energy. He smelt strange as if he had swum in a pool of rum. The blood drops were dripping from the corner of his brow, making their way to the lips to resurrect his dead spirit. The man would stop after every few minutes to prevent his lungs from collapsing

There was a small bulge on the right side of his chest. His arm was bending as if it was serving as a cradle for an infallible creature. A small boy was resting peacefully in his arms. The man would remove his coat every other while to get a glimpse of the boy. After stumbling and tottering, he reached an empty wooden carriage. He looked at it as if it served the sight of relief to him. He hopped on the carriage and decided to let the night finish without any more mystery.

Suddenly, the man started getting restless as the carriage got under the influence of a cunning presence, it toppled, and a loud thud echoed across the town. He started panting. He left the carriage and started running towards an unidentified destination. He kept looking back with eyes that were complaining about the never-ending night. A man shouted from the back,

> "Stop you rascal! I will shoot you if you don't stop."

The man drifted towards a small lane. His eyes were filled with rage. They were giving a deadly look to the innocent being in his arms. The boy had comfortably fallen asleep again in the warm quilt he was wrapped in. The lane was ending with a tall wall. The man holding the baby was only a few inches away from the point of the gun held by the man chasing him.

"Stop before I pull the trigger. Give up on whatever you are thinking of, otherwise, I will get you a dreadful end."

"Do you want this boy, huh? You deprived me of the love of my life. You stabbed me with a sharp burning rod and pierced my heart. Do you know what love can make you do—?"

"Stop, I say stop! For heaven's sake, let's resolve the matter here. You can kill me, but please, don't harm my son."

"It was this boy who sucked my soul out of me. I am already dead. How can I let my soul enter a new body molded of the clay which has specks of impurity extracted from the existence of the world's filthiest being, a betrayer? This story was supposed to meet a tragic end at my hands, so here I am, doing my piece of work."

The man impulsively took a knife out of his coat, held the helpless creature with utter cruelty in his hand, and without a single thought pierced the pure cloak draping the small chest. He mercilessly stabbed the baby and twisted the knife 41 times. The body of the father was struck with a great shock and under the influence of the rage spreading in his body, he fired all the bullets at the man but the knife kept getting twisted in the chest until it got stuck in the fragile ribs. The father squealed and fell as if his body crumbled to non-existence. Humanity witnessed the worst satanic crime that night. The earth felt a tremble and the air blew a huge cry that took over all the streets, roads, and deserted pieces of land.

The bed started shaking violently. Dwayne pushed the quilt off his body with his full strength and immediately burst into tears. His heart felt as if it was ripped from his chest. His breaths were so deep that he could feel his diaphragm touching his lungs. It took him fifteen minutes to distinguish reality from his dream. He tucked his head between his knees and would start whimpering after every other minute. The warmth of humanity radiating in the air kept penetrating his body and was at work to relieve his heart of the stress.

After making sense of everything, he poured himself some water and gulped it down. Every sip felt like a relief from the strain that the chest was putting on his heart. Ulva was still lying next to him as if she intended to wake up late. Dwayne caught sight of the clock and it was already getting late for his work. He decided not to disturb Ulva and make breakfast himself. It had been a long time since he cooked.

He reached the shelf of the kitchen but his head felt heavy. After taking a few steps into the kitchen, he vomited. He was feeling weak. His knees were unable to bear his weight. The room was changing its dimensions for him. It was clear that he was hallucinating. He tried to grab the ingredients out of the fridge but every time he would move his hand forward, he would fall short of getting hold of anything. He spilled everything on himself and passed out.

Ulva was holding a phone close to her ear, and tears were rolling down her cheeks when Dwayne opened his eyes. The moment he regained consciousness, he felt as if something sharp was pressing his skull. When he touched his forehead with his rigid fingers, he saw blood dripping down his brow.

"Am I alright? I guess I am. Umm, I was feeling — I don't know what I was feeling but nothing seemed alright before." Dwayne started talking to himself in a weak voice.
"Yeah, he woke up. Thank you very much. Yeah, I don't need any help now, I will clean him and give him some medicine. If needed, I will bring him to the hospital."

Ulva quickly disconnected the call and rushed towards the kitchen from the corner of the lounge.

"Darling, are you ok? Ah, I got scared—"

Dwayne tried to stand up but he kept slipping. He was getting pale. His tongue was uttering sounds as if he had to say something but the voice sounded weak.

"Don't try too much. You have gotten minor injuries, let me clean them"

Ulva tried to make Dwayne stand, and after multiple efforts, she managed to take him to the lounge. She kept wiping the wounds and sobbing along the process. Her hands were trembling as she was so much concerned about Dwayne's condition.

"Oh darling, I can't wrap my head around it. You were all fine yesterday, how can you possibly fall so sick," she said quietly, "I am bringing you medicine, you better rest till then."

Ulva was stressed about the situation and she was doing everything to serve Dwayne. Her worries were accompanied by her dreadful habit of over thinking. That day felt like the worst one to her. She was scared that she might lose Dwayne. There was no one else in this world whom she could look up to. After making Dwayne sleep comfortably, she went out to her balcony and started reminiscing about the wonderful memories of her life. The vows she had taken while getting married to Dwayne, started getting whispered by some invisible creatures in her ears. The perfume which she had applied brought back memories of her fifth anniversary. She would apply the perfume only when her heart would get flooded with extreme emotions for her beloved husband. The smell was making her blush and smile, as it reminded her of the strange warmth generated each time both souls would find a way to get infused into each other. Then she got the reminiscence of her rousing sex memories with Dwayne. The thought of the sudden rush of Dwayne's bodily fluids in her lower abdomen, flowing through her cervix followed by her intense moans, made her giggle. Within a few minutes, she found herself rubbing her vulva, but she immediately stopped because Dwayne woke up and started calling her name in a quivering voice.

She took care of Dwayne to the fullest and he recovered quickly. Dwayne forgot the dream within a few days and started doing better after that.

9, January

The weather was cold as the winters were seeing their peak. The air that blew would strike everybody like needles. The streets looked lifeless. This city would already seem cursed, winters made it worse. Dwayne took out all the crippled receipts from his drawer to start˙ his monthly calculations. Lethargy was making him slow up day by day. His stamina had started to diminish to its new lows. After managing to complete the calculations within an hour, he started searching for his phone. Dwayne had started seeing the effects of memory loss. He had begun to forget important things around which his life would usually revolve. It took him a couple of minutes to figure out the exact location of his phone.

> "Here you are. My old ass was searching for you everywhere except here." He pulled out his phone after reaching for it in his coat.

The back of the phone was almost falling apart. The plastic cover looked decades old. He turned on the phone. The moment he saw the home interface of his phone, his complacent expression was immediately replaced by a questioning look. There were 9 unread messages. They were from a random number with a different city code. The messages had some unfamiliar and strange content. Dwayne first thought that these texts were meant for someone else, but the queer images attached to them started putting his long-term memory at work.

—What did you think? Would I forget what you did to me? You bloody butcher—

Dwayne was unexpectedly calm after reading this message as he was still expecting them to be mistakenly sent to him.

—You Fuckster, have you ever imagined what it feels like to lose a loved one? I wish I could cast spells on your filthy blood, but unfortunately, I don't have access to them—

—Watch out!!!! I might be quite close to you. Don't let my phone number deceive you—

The other messages were sent after some break. Dwayne noted the time difference and it was of two hours. Dwayne kept re-reading the texts until he started feeling dizzy. By this time, he was trying to read between the lines and brainstorm to find out the potential sender. He immediately found himself a chair to sit in because the anxiety was kicking in. He hadn't downloaded the pictures yet as he feared seeing something triggering.

—I thought these texts would be enough to whoop your old ass but you seem quite tough. Well, you are trying your best to test my patience but I won't let you do it—

—Well, let me make it simple for you. I have kidnapped your daughter. You might have been searching for her for years, but she is with me! She is still alive but I can't guarantee how long she would survive—

Dwayne was stunned after reading these words. Everything had started to become blurry for him. He turned off the phone to take a break. It was almost 6 pm. He grabbed a can of fizzy drink from his neighboring shop and started strolling in front of his pharmacy. There were no customers to deal with so he was utilizing the time to brood over the texts that he had received.

After half an hour, he came back to his pharmacy and mustered up his courage to read the texts again.

—Poor she. She thinks that I love her. I don't! In fact, I hate her. With all my might and main. She thinks we are still friends like we used to be in our childhood. She is mistaken; this is a suffering that I chose for her because of her father's mistake—

—You know what, I have already started poisoning her. She is slowly driving insane. I will make her suffer until she dies. Will we get a reunion at her funeral? It will be a delightful experience to see you dressed in black clothes. I might love seeing your ugly face but it has to be mourning—

Dwayne was getting nervous while reading every single word. He was trying to convince himself that these messages were meant for someone else as he had no daughter. He had never witnessed anything like this in his past so it was difficult for him to believe what he had read.

—I am more than sure that you are reading my texts. You must still act cowardly as you used to before. I am telling you again, there is no way you can stop me. It is confirmed that your daughter will get death as a gift for surviving these four years with me, but you too better watch out—

—Thank me later for giving you a trigger warning but the pictures attached below have your sedated daughter crumbling in a chair. She has been lately begging for death. Don't worry, I will grant her peace very soon—

Dwayne downloaded the images with trembling fingers. Against his expectations, they had nothing triggering. They were capturing an empty rocking chair infested with termites.

A few minutes later, Dwayne got hit by some realization and he started panicking. He recalled something that was triggered by those images and immediately deleted the texts. He turned off his phone impulsively. He wanted to reach his home as early as possible because he feared that he might get a heart attack. The tears of fear were at work to numb his intellect.

7

THE FOURTH SYMBOL

I still got the blurry vision, the vision that on its own can make me forget how to sleep, and the vision that is enough to make someone's life a living hell. Me running down an ugly and wrecked colosseum. The smell was making me lose consciousness after every few minutes. I was trying to wipe the blurring sheath webbing my eyes but was unable to control my body. It felt as if I was controlled by some remote force. My toes were bleeding as the only thing I remember doing was running. My toenails got plucked while I ran over the bed of thorns. Was it a sign that I will be going to hell? Was it a prediction of my future? Nothing made and makes sense. I could see my veins oozing blood into my tissues. The sound of my heartbeat was more than any sound in my surroundings. But there was something strange, I could cry and this was luckily in my control. My heart felt as if it was aching from a heartbreak. My throat was painful and sore. My tongue was heavy and I could barely touch the walls of my mouth with it. My nerves were betraying me but my hormones were the savior.

It took me a couple of minutes to realize that I was running to save myself. It was a fight for survival. The fight that could spare anyone with a life. I don't remember myself seeing behind, but there was a black shadow draping everything with its cunning blackness. It was such a long run that my muscles felt as if they were about to get detached from my bones. Then finally, my legs led me to an empty dark room. They stopped as if they wanted to show me something. I tried to look around but my body wasn't in my control. The warm tears were losing their identity in the sweat. I was drenched with blood, sweat, and tears. My body was about to explode because my hormones wanted to take over. It felt like a rivalry between my nerves and hormones.

After that, I was waiting for a horse to come and accept me as its master. I wanted someone to get hold of me. I was all alone. It brought back memories from the time when I was all alone after Dad's death. At that time, I was waiting for someone to be my companion, although it was impossible to find a substitute for him.

There has to be a hole in every window that sneaks the light of hope into your life, and I was in search of it. I started to accept my defeat and I let my body loose so it could surrender to these events. My clothes started to dissolve into the pores of my body. After a few minutes, I was standing in the middle of an empty room that couldn't even give shelter to my body and my soul.

The moment I inoculated the feeling of defeat in my heart, my warm tears started healing the very points they fell on. My wounds started getting wiped and the tears started regenerating the crusts of my toenails. I wanted to smile at this little light of hope, but alas, my body was not in my control.

These feelings of victory didn't last for quite long. Something started to pull every ligament in my body again and I started running. But this time, the journey felt different as if my legs wanted to show me something meaningful. Finally, I reached my destination, which was a beautiful garden. I opened the gate with my trembling hands. The door was covered in ivies and lilies. I wanted to touch them and smell them, but alas, my body was still not in my control. However, I wasn't feeling destitute anymore because I was expecting to come across a beacon of hope. The gate opened and it felt as if a bubble bearing heavenly scent exploded. I could smell jasmine. The grass was moist. The dew drops started taking into them all the accumulated tiredness in me. This was the time when my brain started observing everything in the surroundings, in order to extract the hidden message.

The newly bloomed flowers were telling me that spring had recently arrived. This world seemed perfect to me. I requested God to stay there because this place made me feel owned. The colors were getting infused into my dead soul. People wrongly attribute red as the color of love, purple feels more royal. I saw heavenly flowers hanging in the garden. I wanted to touch them and smell them but my body was still not in my control. The flapping love birds were forming a trail over the garden. I was always told that animals serve beautiful princesses, but this time it was a guy being served like a snow white. I was wondering what would happen if my body was in my control this whole time. Would my body still bring me here? I bet not. We have narrow brains, a little suffering can illude our minds.

I wish I had wished for something else. A white horse came near me and it was there to reveal the hidden secrets of the garden. I was shown many wonders after riding it. I wanted to bow in respect before the creator of this garden. Who could it be? We humans are so self-praising that we never even attempt to lead the quest to find the real creator. We count worldly wonders as the only mesmerizing spectacles. It was so difficult to not get lost in the enchantments of the garden, however, a part of me was in search of my loved ones. I was somehow expecting to find them there.

No matter what we perceive, there always has to be a veil that can deceive us. We think that beauty is the only parameter to measure goodness. It takes a great amount of courage to accept the fact that ugly things have the most beautiful cores. It has to be Satan who deceives us, otherwise, God never discriminated between beauty and ugliness. I heard the sound of some bird flapping its wings in the water. This was something that sank my heart for good's sake. I was expecting a beautiful water body to be quite near me. Counting the beauty of the garden, anyone would have expected the mesmerizing sight of a river or lake. Therefore, the more that horse took me close to the lake, the more butterflies I was getting in my stomach. My breath was smelling sweet as if happiness was doing its magic inside me. I was preparing my body to get stunned by the beauty of the creatures that I was about to see. After a few minutes, a sound filled the domes of my eyes with tears. Although the blurring sheath was still there to deceive my sight, the tears somehow penetrated that sheath. I started seeing everything. I didn't know that a cry of a swan would make me regain my consciousness. I finally got triumphant and won control of my body. The cry of that swan made me fall from the horse, and I rushed towards the bush that was standing between me and that lake.

When I reached the place, my hands impulsively made their way to my chest and I wanted to put my heart to sleep. The sight was nothing less than heartbreaking. The lake was expectedly beautiful, but the beauty was just an illusion. The surface of the body was hidden under the canopy of purple aconites. The flowers had a butterfly-like appearance. This excitement was nothing in front of the emotion of bereavement. Many swans were lying dead, with their wings fully spread, near the lake. A bewitching smell was making me dizzy. The trees near the lake had lowered their branches pointing towards the river. I rushed towards one swan. I had never seen such a helpless creature ever in my life. I took it in my arms and burst into tears. The blood mixed with the tears was dripping under the force of gravity onto my bare thighs. It felt as if I had lost a loved one. The heartbreak was so gruesome that my cry echoed in the garden. I was almost stunned when my cry sounded like that of a swan. I passed out immediately after this.

I woke up with my toes touching the petals of aconite in the river. I could feel the petals emptying their poison into the pores of my toes.

The trees were doing their work, stirring the drops of hate potion in the river. By now, there were 40 swans dead around me. I had to be the 41st. When I saw my arms, they had transformed into charming wings. I touched my beak and my head had an appealing crown adjusted on it. I had realized by now that I was the king in this land. My faithful servants had poisoned themselves to save me from the curse. They preferred death rather than letting me die, but little did they know that I too would be lying peacefully in my royal casket soon.

Something grabbed my feet; I was dragged into the lake. My wings couldn't bear my weight because the pull from the water was making their efforts go to waste. The water started turning red and then I heard a plop, and the water immediately turned black. I didn't want to leave a story of dishonoring death. Before the potion of hate could make everyone in the bevy disappointed, I pushed one aconite down my throat and chose the death of sacrifice. Now, the count rose to 41.

We don't often realize that we are going to be a part of bigger or smaller legends. We have to leave a legacy behind, and sometimes it is important to sacrifice our existence for the sake of leaving a beacon of hope. Not all stories have a complete ending.

Vernon closed his diary. He was heavy with his thoughts. The dream had left him bewildered. He was trying to get control of the reins of his life but the only thing he gained was pain. He was in search of love, he felt deprived. The emotions were getting overbearing for him. He couldn't figure out the things that he wanted. He just wanted things to get sorted on their own but life was cruel to him. His body was under the influence of regret, anger, sadness, anxiety, and fatigue. By now, he had realized that he was on his own. Although he was trying his best to find support in the form of Willa, things didn't seem to change. He had started taking out his childhood clothes to somehow fit into them. His childhood is what made his regrets weigh more.

Every time he wanted to stand from his chair, some memory would pound him back as if his body wanted him to pen down all the grievances on a piece of paper. He went to his kitchen and prepared himself an appetizing dinner. He left broccoli in water to get it boiled. He took his food outside and sat facing the moon. The moonlight was making his tears sparkle like crystals. He could foresee things getting worse in the near future. That dream too had sewed some of the most cherished lessons to his heart. The number 41 was moving back and forth in his brain. He knew the number before too but had forgotten the context. He would stop after taking every bite in hope that something in his surroundings would remind him about its significance. His depressed eyes were in search of some ray of hope. His ears were eager to hear the voice of his savior. Heavy with depressing thoughts, he slept outside. The dream had gotten so deeply engraved on his brain that he had forgotten about Willa, as his worries were his new partner.

Vernon got himself used to a new habit. He would go out and jog in his street. He would do it to divert his mind from the worries that were eating him up like termites. Dawn was his new favorite time to jog. He liked the aroma of leaves holding freshly exuded dew drops. The chirp of birds was the morning song that he would listen to daily. It had been a week since he saw that dream. The grave seriousness of the symbolism in it had been making him uneasy. He got to witness multiple revelations too so it was a lot for him to handle. He almost stopped his quest to find the meanings of the hidden messages because of a strange feeling invading his existence. He felt as if death was approaching him. The weird thing was that he was excited to embrace death. He had come to terms with the fact that he had nothing worthy to live for.

Vernon rushed into his room. He slammed

the door with full force. He dragged the chair in front of his writing table to find his diary. He searched everywhere but the diary was missing. He destroyed everything that came into his way. The rage was so frightening that the curtains hid the scene from the outside world because it could terrorize any creature. Vernon took a knife and tore open his bed. He wanted to find his diary in any case. His body was burning with the fire of revenge. His heart wanted him to do something that could cause havoc. He had a look of betrayal in his eyes. He was panting so loudly that its sound was louder than that of the destruction he was causing.

"Willa? Where are you?" he screamed at the top of his lungs.

There was no response. He broke into the washroom and every single room that he could find in that house, but he couldn't find her.

"Come out or I will harm myself. Look, I have this sharp baby in my hand, it can easily pierce my carotid artery. Do you want to live the rest of your life alone?" Vernon shouted while holding the knife close to his neck. His mouth had begun foaming.
"Where is my diary? I know you read it and you are hiding it from me. You betrayer! You traitor! I will fucking kill you—."

Still, there was no response. He once again started the search for his diary. This time, he was searching for it under the influence of fear. A fear that somebody might reveal his reality. A reality, that he didn't even know himself. He always had this concern that somebody might declare him insane, and he would get sent to an asylum. He thought that he would die if he ever got to live a lonely life again. He searched everywhere, in every room, but all to no avail. He accidentally cut his three fingers with the sharp knife. He didn't care about the wounds, although the pain was intense. He had only two things in his head: his struggle to save his future and hiding his reality.

He finally gave up on the search. He looked hopeless and started hurting himself. This time, he was taken over by the emotions of fear, loneliness, sadness, and mistrust. He was sure that Willa was behind this act of betrayal. He started cursing himself for letting others exploit him. He tucked his head between his legs and started crying vehemently. He cried like a child. He had forgotten about his wounds. He just wanted to cry his heart out. While crying, that dream started flashing before his eyes. The heartbreak followed by death, the self-chosen death, appeared in front of his eyes. He picked up the knife and swung his arm towards his chest to end his life but someone grabbed his arm. His helpless expression got substituted by the emotion of disbelief. He tried to look at the person but his eyes were unable to catch a glimpse, because of his dizzy head. After this failed attempt, he immediately passed out.

8

THE FIFTH SYMBOL

12, January

The rocks were shockingly soft. They were getting trampled under her hoofs. Ulva was standing at the base of a mighty mountain. The appearance of the mountain was less rocky and more of a hill. A beautiful falling stream could be seen erupting out of it. The water was somehow disappearing at the foot of the mountain, thus startling its possible spectators. The water was so crystal clear that the cave opening behind that stream could be clearly seen witnessing for its purity, a purity that was getting impacted even by the slightest of the colors in the surroundings. Ulva moved towards the stream with a cautious gait. Her life experiences had already taught her a lesson that the things that visibly look appealing aren't necessarily valuable.

Traps are always waiting for you to make a fool out of yourself and challenge your sanity.

However, Ulva was visibly so bedazzled by the unworldly beauty of this land that she didn't even realize the form she had attained to gain entrance to this world. She was surrounded by so many complexities that she almost forgot to prioritize her focus. She neighed out of shock after realizing that she had transformed into the most magical creature in this world, a Goddess-like unicorn. She could sense the wonders done by her magical body. The hair on her body was exuding its own musk-like scent. One could have assumed that the scent was sent in a wondrous bottle from heaven, but this was what the magic of love and care did to her. She was known in this world as *Aphrodite* "The Goddess of love". This was the first time the universe was witnessing an animal form of Aphrodite.

Ulva was in a state of confusion as it was getting hard for her to decide what she wanted to explore first. The continued confrontations with different attributes of the land kept clouding her mind. She moved closer to the mountain and stuck her tongue out, and took it near its base to taste the water. The body of such a Goddess could do anything, diverting the flow of water was not something unexpected. A few drops fell on her tongue and then turned into a beautiful mist. Its bewitching scent entered her muzzle. She shook her head out of disbelief. She was deeply moved by the spells that were being cast in front of her due to her past acts of sacrifice. The tale of love narrated by her had gotten written in the books in this world, and had become a lesson for every other creature. She was never blamed here for the decisions that she had made in the past. Everyone understood the significance of each step that she had taken, and now, it was time for her to realize how great of an impact she had left through her story.

The surroundings had already started numbing her senses. This world was so unique that even the smallest act of goodness could get written as something magnificent in its history books. The positivity of her surroundings made her pledge to spend the rest of her life under the cloak that shelters all the acts of goodness. It was the time when she realized the grave seriousness of the matter of making the human world a better place. This world seemed more realistic to her because the outcomes of each deed seemed more appropriate. Any evil act would have created the same effect as an act of goodness.

After she got comfortable with her body, she started exploring the wonders of being a heavenly creature. The white on her body was so pure that even the smallest thing that brushed against it could be spotted. Her knee-length white hair kept shining in the sun. Her head had an alluring crown. Even her horn's length carried its own set of explanations. Every tale of Ulva's life was written across each twist of the horn. The language was non-native so she didn't get to read the tales which had created such an impact on this land. She found a tree that had leaves acting as mirrors for her. It was time for Ulva to see her green eyes and a Goddess-like body. The leaves adjusted themselves according to Ulva's height so that she could comfortably bedazzle herself with the beauty she was donning. Ulva's eyes could be seen sparkling with tears of joy. She neighed out of excitement after looking at each magnificent feature her body had attained. Then suddenly, a thought hit her and she galloped back to the foot of the mountain.

This time, a few elves came to escort her to a cave from there. The elves weren't tiny like they are assumed to be in the fairy tales. Each elf had a unique body stature. Finally, she entered a cave. The cave wasn't as attractive as she expected it to be.

> "My dear Goddess, please wait here. You will be taken to your throne. We aren't allowed to go with you," said one of the elves.

The elves left Ulva alone in that small cave. Scented water was dripping from the walls and the air felt moist. Ulva started feeling nauseous. After a brief wait, the other side of the cave opened which led her into a prodigious amphitheater. The walls were tall. The place had no light except a small gap in the roof that was serving as an entrance for an intense beam. Later, Ulva felt as if her thighs were getting moist with some exudation. When she looked back, her anal region was secreting a gooey liquid. The smell was noticeable and unexpectedly fragrant. The liquid kept dripping down her thighs. She was getting disgusted but the smell was compelling her to think the other way. This didn't stop here as she suddenly started feeling intense pleasure in her lower region. The feeling was so intense that she bent her forelegs out of the ecstasy running down her body. She closed her eyes because she could feel every muscle of her body getting contracted.

The later events deluded her mind to a greater extent. She noticed many male unicorns coming out of the doors of the amphitheater. Their heads could be seen bowing from respect. She was unable to comprehend the situation. Nevertheless, the feeling of ecstasy was so strong that she said something to them that later made her regret it.

> "Who wants to mate with me?" She blurted out loudly. Her dialogue echoed throughout the amphitheater.

Everyone lifted their heads from shock. There was

silence for a few moments.

Then one managed to speak and said, "I beg your pardon, but it is you who has to decide the partner for this holy affair. We, your servants, are waiting for your commandment. We were told that the queen is going to mate today so we all gathered here."

Ulva was confused for a few moments, but the condition she was in kept instigating her to make the decision quickly.

"You! The one with golden reins, follow me!" Ulva commanded one of them.

This unicorn was a sturdy one and black in color. He was known for his anger. Many would avoid messing with him because of his narcissistic attitude. He was hesitant in following the Queen.

"You are commanded by the Goddess to follow her to her throne room! Who can dare to challenge her commandments? Have you forgotten her sacrifices for this land?" said one of them.

The chosen one butted the other unicorn out of anger. Ulva turned to see but she noticed nothing significant, so she continued walking. They both entered a room that was decorated with alluring flowers. The floor felt as if an expensive velvet mat had been spread to grant the preparations an appropriate amount of royalness. The male unicorn didn't look much interested in the details. Ulva removed her crown. She got herself comfortable and laid on the throne that caught her sight. She adjusted her forelegs carefully in the sieves prepared for them. After a few minutes of the adjustment, she stopped producing the sweetly scented liquid. She used her tongue to clean the liquid off her body because her partner looked disgusted. He was hesitating in advancing towards her. He somehow wanted to hurt her feelings.

> "You can leave if you want to. I will ask someone else," said the queen in a gentle voice after a few minutes of waiting.

He stayed silent for some time and then decided to obey the queen. The moment he entered the queen's body, she neighed once again out of intense pleasure. It started making her thighs twitch, her forelegs stretch to the fullest, and her muscles relax. Due to the roughness of her partner, the sieves fixing her hoofs got pulled out of their place and the room started echoing with sounds of clattering metal. The thrusts kept painfully hitting her clitoris till she used her legs to support her body and make her partner stop. This made her body relax for a while. However, the rest was followed by a sudden wave of shiver that ran down her body, as she started sensing something strange around her. When she looked back, her partner's eyes were filled with rage. They were turning red and the veins around his horn were getting visible. The thriving blood in those veins was making his skin palpitate. He tried to stab her with his pointed horn but another unicorn suddenly rushed in to protect the queen. The queen survived the murder attempt. Her eyes looked stunned. They captured a look that explained the resonation of a certain past trauma with this event. Her green eyes no longer looked brighter as they had turned gloomy. She felt betrayed.

This was the first heartbreak of the evening that made her feel miserable, as all the marvels that she had already seen lost their worth after this moment.

Ulva was convinced by now that the beauty of the captivating worlds can't neutralize the coexisting evils. She had trusted the wrong beings in the human world, and a certain filter deceived her in this world too. Later, that unicorn got trampled to death by all the unicorns and was hanged as a lesson in the amphitheater. Every time Ulva would catch sight of him, a strange pain would make her heart sink, eventually getting her teary-eyed. But she had to move on and she tried.

The one who saved her was her old lover. He loved her madly and even after seeing the love of his life with someone else, he was determined to protect the queen.

> "I know I hurt you. I am sorry, I was losing control of my body at that time and I thought he could fulfill my physical needs." Ulva summoned him and apologized.
>
> "No need to do it, my dear queen. I am your servant and I have no right to complain."

Ulva rubbed her muzzle against his body. They kept looking into each other's eyes, and the tension building between both of them started making up for the evils of the day.

21, January

Ulva was greatly influenced by this journey which she experienced in her dream. It felt as if her life was summarized in an enchanting way. The sacrifices she had made, the emotions she had to go through in her life, and the tale that she had to lead, everything was brought back to her in the form of a dream. There were still some lessons that she needed to learn, so they got closure in that sequence. The fact that flares of magic can get ignited by showing love, got summed up for her realistically in that dream. It kept playing a symphony in her ears, trying to tell her that what she had done in her life was something that nobody else would even have the courage to do. She was tested uniquely and the solutions which she came up with, were quite intricately managed.

27, January

"It can't be him. No, I know it isn't him."

Dwayne kept mumbling in his sleep. The shock caused by seeing the messages that he received a few days ago, had started haunting him in his dreams too. The rocking chair he saw in the pictures kept putting great strain on his brain. He was suspecting one person to be the potential sender of those texts, but he knew the nature of that boy. Hatred could never become the way for him to convey his message.

Dwayne's health started deteriorating once again. He kept getting weaker day by day. His food portions had started to get smaller too. The only thing he would think of was consuming a disastrous amount of alcohol. Most of the time, he would come back drunk from his work. Ulva was quite concerned about his condition. Her unexplainable love was making her make such compromises. She was taking in all the hate that Dwayne was targeting at her, as she knew something was bothering him. He had never acted like this before so it was evident that something ugly had started making his life nightmarish. She feared that hatred would get between them, eventually making this relationship toxic, but she wholeheartedly accepted this new dynamic of her life as her fate because she didn't want to give up on him.

However, domestic abuse was the only thing that she was scared of. She knew that this could rot her relationship to the core. She avoided talking to Dwayne to prevent any complications. She knew that even the slightest jerk from him could make her hate him forever. She was ready to compromise for any other kind of distancing in her relationship, but she wasn't ready for this. Some traumas associated with this dynamic of a relationship scared her of the consequences following it.

Ulva had been a woman of principles. She understood very well that these times were scary and difficult, but she had to make the odds work for her. The companionship of about 9 years was something that kept her from finding flaws in Dwayne. Even Dwayne was trying to keep himself in control, but things weren't working for either of them as they wanted. Both of them were occupied with their thoughts, worries, and concerns. Both had a different but ugly past. This was making their present insufferable. Ulva would usually feel like a wounded bird. She would often try to question her fate, but the good times that she had spent with Dwayne would stop her from being ungrateful. Every single wrinkle on her face reminded her that she had come this far all because of her immense courage, and that she had to move forward.

Dwayne would look at the moon and often get lost in the bewitching hue fading the moonlight. How good were the times when we had each other and there was no one else to bother us? He would often think about this question. He was quite happy to have Ulva in his life, but the worries were making it difficult for him to survive.

What possibly changed the time so much? This ugly present, is it a curse or karma? These thoughts were lately bothering Ulva too. Sometimes when Dwayne would make an effort to listen to her carefully, she would ask him these questions. She was worried about the possible consequences that could have been caused by certain decisions that they took in the past. Maybe they had unintentionally ruined someone's life, and this was making their life uneasy was the thought she would often get. At night, Dwayne would put his head in Ulva's lap to make an attempt at melting down the blinding sheath stopping the two hearts from getting along with each other. This would be followed by an expression of remorse where both of them would sob for hours. They just wanted these difficult times to end soon.

28, January

Ulva was going through the list of possible dishes that she could prepare for her anniversary. It was the day she wanted to make memorable for herself, as it marked the completion of a decade of her marriage. She had bought herself an intricately tailored dress for the date night she was going to have with Dwayne. The dress fitted her waist with ultimate perfection, while her broad hips cushioned its edges in a glamorizing way. Her decently visible bosom and perfectly symmetrical face kept making her look like a supreme Goddess, especially the Goddess of piety. It was one of the rare times when she wore the diamond necklace given by her mother. She wanted to make Dwayne feel special, so she donned everything that made her look nothing less than royalty.

Ulva had bought Dwayne a suit too. She replaced the buttons on the sleeves with expensive studs that contrasted well with the suit's navy blue color. She sprayed an expensive musk on the coat that she had bought for him on some other anniversary. She placed the oud at the entrance of her house. Its aroma spread everywhere inside.

Ulva had prepared everything and the table was ready. She was waiting for Dwayne. She was expecting him to come, take a shower and change clothes, but she waited for hours and there were no signs of him coming any sooner.

It was already midnight and Ulva had fallen asleep on the table. Her hair had gone messy, and her makeup had gotten smudged as if she had cried before falling asleep. At two o'clock, someone rang the bell. Ulva opened the door enthusiastically, but she was disappointed when she saw a man trying to keep Dwayne standing upright. He was visibly drunk. Ulva made him settle on the sofa. Dwayne saw the preparations on the table and understood the context even after being drunk. Then he said something hurtful that made Ulva question her conscience for a second.

"You ugly lady! You really thought that I would be celebrating our anniversary?" He rolled his eyes and mumbled.

After hearing these degrading remarks, Ulva rushed to her room and slammed the door. She immediately burst into tears. She was heartbroken that all her efforts went in vain. She had started believing by now that Dwayne was cheating on her. She had a firm belief that a man who would once admire her for her beauty, was seeing someone more appealing than her, and that's why he had started seeing flaws in her. There was nothing that could make her stop wailing. Dwayne was drunk so he didn't pay much attention to the crying sounds. Ulva ripped her dress out of the pain she felt after hearing the word 'ugly'. She buried herself in multiple blankets and kept sobbing for the whole night.

29, January

Dwayne went to take a shower. Ulva was still heartbroken and the words were continuously stinging her. She couldn't properly sleep the earlier night. Her eyes looked drowsy, and her body looked distraught. The insult didn't affect her much but the thought of getting cheated was eating her alive. The pain was getting unbearable for her. The regret of spending a decade with a person who could never become her, was killing her and tearing her heart into million pieces.

> "Dwayne, I loved you. I gave you everything. I prioritized you over myself, but my efforts never counted. How can I not get compelled to think that I am making the biggest mistake by staying with you?" mumbled Ulva while tears rolled down her cheeks.

After a few minutes of breakdown, something hit her intuitively and she decided to check Dwayne's phone. When she unlocked the phone, the only thing she could see was the missed calls from her. These were the calls from last night. She sighed from excruciating pain, while tears continued to trickle from the corner of her eyes onto her pillow. She kept mustering up the courage to look further into Dwayne's phone. When she was about to turn it off, Dwayne received a message from an unknown number. The texts didn't stop getting sent. There were a series of texts getting received in batches. Ulva suspected the sender to be the potential person whom Dwayne was in a relationship with. The moment she saw the texts, a strange feeling started pressing her skull. She started trembling out of fear. The reason behind this was not known to her either. When she opened the texts, she couldn't wrap her head around them at the beginning. The texts were hateful but this wasn't something that concerned her. What petrified her the most were the sent pictures reminding her of some ugly memories. She shrieked out of pain. The pain was so intense that she was having difficulty breathing. She had seen something unbearable that made her chest feel heavy. The phone dropped from her hand and she fell to the floor.

Dwayne heard a thud and rushed out of the bathroom. He got struck with an agonizing shock when he saw Ulva in this condition. She was lying on the floor with her eyes wide open. Dwayne saw his phone lying near her. When he picked up the phone, his heart dropped too. The texts weren't something that could have moved them so insanely, it were the photos that wrenched their souls in the most heartbreaking way.

The images had a hand that had deep cuts on the fingers. The bone could be visibly seen, as the knuckles were popping out. The images were triggering, but what followed next made Dwayne's heart stop beating for a few moments. He saw a ring on an injured finger. The ring was something that made Dwayne stumble and eventually drop to his knees. Dwayne wanted the floor to suck him in it. This image was the one that had made Ulva shriek too. The significance of the ring made them recognize the person, and the thought of him getting hurt had left both of them completely distraught. Dwayne swiped his trembling fingers on the screen and cried with a trembling voice. He could feel death approaching him.

9

Vernon had been unconscious for many hours. Plankton was waiting for him to wake up. His spine pain was making him restless but seeing Vernon in such condition worried him more. Vernon's pale body was resting in the crooked bed. He had cried so much that his eyes could be seen to have sunken to a great extent. The white crusty deposits of dried tears had been worsening the wounds formed in the gruesome cracks on his face. His skin had become flaky and dry. The sheets of his bed were torn, and the fine threads were constructing a narrow vent to help Vernon's body escape. Vernon's hands had deep cuts and his neck had faint marks left by the sharp knife. His lips were looking swollen and were turning blue as if they had failed to do one job they were supposed to, calling Willa with all the energy left in his body before he passed out. One of his arms kept hanging from the bed, while the blood from his injured hand continued to drip on the floor. The red flesh, visible from the cracks, was telling Plankton about Vernon's tales of loneliness. He was shocked at his condition because he had never witnessed such an extreme case of depression.

Plankton moved his chair closer to the bed to take a look at the marks on Vernon's body. He started by pulling up his sleeves. The arms had needle holes. The marks had worsened so much that bright bruises were the only thing to be seen instead of his skin. His skin color had faded away to such an extent that it was getting difficult for Plankton to figure out Vernon's actual complexion.

Plankton found an old wooden phonograph in the room. A few music cassettes were lying near it so he decided to play them turn by turn. Each song impacted his intellect in a way that he couldn't stop his heart from shattering. The room too was trying to tell the heart-wrenching tales of Vernon's traumas. The lack of love was depriving all the things of life in his surroundings. After witnessing everything, Plankton was unable to control himself and ended up breaking into tears, while his sobs kept getting louder with each passing moment. The heartbreak Plankton felt was so intense that he could feel his chest getting tight from his wails. This whole time, his head remained bent downwards, while his tears kept drowning his wrecked existence. The loneliness lingering in the air kept creeping into his heart making him feel Vernon's vulnerability in a different way.

Plankton gathered his courage to explore some more marks on Vernon's body. By now, Plankton was convinced that Vernon had been suffering from severe depression for the past few years. He had been hiding his pain and suffering all this time, but somehow his trauma got revealed in front of Plankton. While looking at his body, there was one point that later made Plankton regret looking at because the sight completely stunned him. He saw a heart tattoo on Vernon's left shoulder, and it was bleeding as if he had tried to scratch it off with a sharp object. There were multiple cuts on his back forming sieve-like folds with blood clotted in them. The sight kept getting unbearable for Plankton, while the music was piercing his heart. The choice of music was an explanation in itself of what Vernon had been going through.

The more Plankton looked at his body, the louder the wails kept getting. His sobs were echoing in the house as if everything present in the house was extending their condolences too by weeping with him. The house had some mystic kind of sadness. Plankton didn't have the courage to explore more because of the fear of cunning sadness making his heart stop beating. He was waiting for Vernon to open his eyes but it didn't seem to be happening soon, the body looked too fragile to even try to stand up again.

Around 3 am, Vernon opened his eyes. Plankton had fallen asleep by then in the broken chair near the bed. His body had gotten stiff because of the hours of wait.

"Wat–ee–rrr," Vernon whispered.

The house was so silent that Plankton easily heard Vernon and immediately opened his eyes.

"Ok, water? Ok, let me get it for you." He sounded confused because of the joy he was feeling after seeing Vernon waking again.

Vernon had started doing better in the morning. Plankton brought him breakfast and gave him important medicines. His eyes were still gleaming with the stuck tears, but he looked hopeful. Vernon seemed terrorized too, but he was somehow trying to use his abilities to hide his pain.

Plankton would keep getting impacted by great shock after the reminiscence of the traumatizing events from the previous night. He was trying to make Vernon talk as little as possible; he feared that the already shutting windows of his life could make him lose the battle soon. Thinking about his traumatic past was the last thing Plankton wanted Vernon to do, so he stayed silent.

"I will be checking on you tomorrow. I got some clinic-related work. Take good care of yourself," said Plankton in a gentle voice.

Plankton wore his coat and left. Vernon didn't say anything and kept gazing at the ceiling while lying in his bed. His expression looked stern as if he was unable to comprehend the events revolving around him. He woke up close to sunset. He could see the orange light getting cast by the breathtakingly-beautiful setting sun on the floor of his lounge. He tried to stand up but his legs were too weak to support his body. He knew that he wouldn't be able to make it to witness the sunset, so he instead attempted to reach the food placed on the table standing a few feet away from the bed.

His physical and mental wounds had left him so distraught that he couldn't even think properly. While being stuck in such a situation, he kept looking for Willa because he had almost forgotten about the previous day.

> "Willa, come. The food is here. Plankton brought us something that smells so good." After a small pause, he continued, "I know you are scared that I might hurt you for stealing my diary but I promise that I won't. Come and eat with me, you must have gotten hungry while hiding all day from me."

There were no signs of her existence in the home. Vernon kept his sight steady while expecting her to enter from the door of his room, but he lost his hopes after a few minutes. The disappointment made the food taste bitter to him. He expected Willa to reappear while taking each bite but the house just had two residents, him and his loneliness. Later after getting done, he went back to his bed and tried to fall asleep. His body was in severe pain by now; lethargy was making every single wound hurt more.

Vernon suddenly woke up in the middle of the night. He was feeling thirsty and scared. The moment he opened his eyes, he was taken over by an amplifying shock. He found Willa lying next to him. His heart started racing from fear after looking at her body which looked like a corpse. The feeling of petrification was quickly replaced by excitement and then by anger: the anger for her not being with him when he needed her the most, the anger for stealing the most important thing from him, the anger for trying to expose him to the world, the anger for the betrayal, the anger for taking advantage of his trust, the anger for leaving him to die, the anger for not being the healing for his wounds recently, and the anger for not being a good companion in these times. But the anger was once again taken over by complete sadness, the sadness over not having a trustworthy human in his life. Even after making so many sacrifices, even after spending his life in deprivation, and even after so much suffering, he had nobody to tell him that everything would get better. But later, he started reminiscing about the great memories that he had made with Willa: the times when she was quite faithful to him and would make him feel special, beloved, and owned, and the times when she played her role of the motherly figure. She had been there for him but he was neglecting her contributions. Maybe her fear was stopping her from protecting him this time; these were the thoughts that started making love sprout again in his heart. Out of excitement, he made an attempt to kiss her on the cheek but his body still felt vulnerable.

Suddenly, his lower body started feeling numb. He was losing sensation in his limbs. He was unable to comprehend the root cause and by the time he started cursing his fate again, he lost consciousness and fell into his bed. The quilt adjusted itself on his body as if somebody was keeping an eye on him from heaven, and the night continued as usual.

Within a week, Vernon started getting better. He started going for jogs in the morning. He started relishing sunsets. He once again began to try to get along with humans. His trust issues were getting resolved with each passing day. His body wasn't in agony anymore. His flesh had started filling his wounds. In short, hope started looking back at him with a sympathetic eye and this somehow made his future look less bleak for a while. He was grateful for the helping hand that Plankton extended to him. He had started developing immense respect for him. Finally, he was able to fathom the decree hidden in the events happening around him. He once again started to look forward to seeing the positive aspects of life. He no longer felt vulnerable and fortunately, he had stopped his preparations to make his way to the linen-lined casket.

However, Plankton stopped visiting him after some time. Vernon thought that he must have been busy with his clinic. He had already done quite a lot for him and thus he had no complaints. The care that Plankton had provided reminded Vernon of his dad and for this, he owed him a lot. He stopped thinking much about it and started focusing on his recovery.

10

THE SEVENTH SYMBOL

30, January

Ulva closed her eyes but she couldn't sleep. The image would start getting painted in front of her the moment she would shut her eyes. The picture was making her restless, while the pain was suffocating her. She was regretful too as if some truth had been unveiled at the wrong time. A new symphony was getting orchestrated after the revelation. The ring she saw had a far-reaching impact on her heart. It was late for her and Dwayne to take any step because they wanted to avoid any more suffering, but they knew it too that some of their past decisions had unwantedly generated a disastrous impact.

The night following the soul-wrenching revelations felt like the longest. Dwayne had been lying restlessly, while his soul wanted to sneak out of his body. The guilt was driving him crazy. Both of them didn't even get time to console each other, because their individual heartbreak was already making them lose their identity. Both of them had different thoughts about the unfolding of truth. Ulva didn't get the chance to explain her intentions. Dwayne wasn't disappointed; he was just cursing the narrow-mindedness that had made him take certain steps in the past. The trails of their tears were leaching into the fine threads of the bed weaving a new tale. Their hearts were heavy. The hopelessness was compelling them to think about dying. They knew that there was no going back to the times when things could get resolved, and this thought was making their lives even more unbearable.

However, Ulva somehow believed in her heart that her past decisions were intelligently measured. At that time, the dungeons of helplessness had been getting darker each day and she considered those decisions to be the only way to light the beacon of hope. The walls used to smell rotten and kindness was something that she considered the appropriate potion to neutralize the poisonous smell. The grooves would echo with fear and a humane decision was what could fix it. She felt as if she had been stabbed in her heart because of the sudden revelation of her secret, but she believed that with each passing day, things would get back to normal. The gentle harp kept getting played in her ears trying to pacify her heart. Her body was trying to make her feel ok because every single element of nature knew that what she had done in her past, was going to become a lesson for many in the future.

Ulva kept waking up in the middle of the night to prevent her throat from drying up, because her chest had been burning with the fire of restlessness. She didn't even know what she could possibly do to speed up the process of progress toward peace. Her body felt as if it was slowly preparing itself for a difficult future. Her heart wanted to give her some hope, but her brain was giving her the signals that she had to muster up the courage for witnessing the hardest times that humanity would ever get to see. This life was not for her, she was in search of love but the real purpose of her getting sent to the world was something else. Although she was silently revered by the elements of nature, she still had to take a sip from the bowl filled with a bitter potion that would make her lose many beloved things.

Ulva woke up suddenly in the morning. Her arms felt numb and she was feeling nauseous. Her mouth was dry and even the air rushing down her breathing passages kept stinging her throat like needles. She found Dwayne still sleeping next to her, although it was already late for him to go to his pharmacy. When Ulva tried to wake him up, she got the sensation that his body was burning with a fever. His cheeks had sunken and his ears were turning red. His body was bending inwards as if his muscles had gotten too weak to hold his body together.

Ulva gave him some medicines and prepared the food that she thought would help Dwayne gain back his energy. He didn't utter a single word and kept staring at his lap while Ulva spoon-fed him. His body would get sudden jolts followed by him sweating profusely. Ulva kept wiping the sweat appearing on his forehead. She even called a doctor but he hadn't arrived yet. During this time, she would hide in the washroom for a few minutes just to spare herself some time to cry her heart out.

Dwayne started showing some progress after a few hours, but still, there was no conversation between the two. Ulva kept making rounds of the house to provide Dwayne with everything that he needed. She was trying her best to hide her heartbreak from him. She knew that he was equally heartbroken but the confrontation of two heartbroken souls would get even more painful, so she kept making things look normal. During this time, she was planning something too, after all, she was restless to stop things from getting diverted to a narrow lane with a dreadful end. She knew that someone needed her the most, but Dwayne's situation was bothering her more. She was stuck once again but she didn't want to delay things any further.

Later that night, Ulva sat close to the balcony while drinking her tea. The lights were turned off because she was gazing at the bright moon. She was expecting someone else to be looking at the moon too, that's why she wanted to connect to him this way. The moonlight falling on her face kept revealing her majestic beauty. Her hair could be seen emitting a fiery light just like a Goddess. The moonlight kept healing some of her shallow wounds.

Suddenly, she started smelling something pungent. Dwayne was resting in his room so her instincts made her rush toward it, but Dwayne was lying peacefully in his bed. After a few minutes of searching, she found a dead cat on her balcony. Ulva got teary after seeing this because the thought of losing everything linked to her, started killing her from the inside. Her soul felt a sudden tremble and her heart felt sinking. She held the cat in her lap for a few minutes and wept. This cat would always be there to make Ulva feel owned, and would never leave her alone. Although the first few interactions had been scary for Ulva, but later, she got along with her. Ulva decided to bury the cat in her courtyard.

Her clothes had gone muddy from a pure crescent-like white while burying her. Her collarbone had become wet from the sinking tears that were trying to trespass the sheath surrounding her heart to console her. Ulva checked on Dwayne once again before falling asleep and his fever had gotten better. She closed her eyes and let her body surrender so nature could once again start pacifying her. She was waiting for a divine revelation because it was getting almost impossible for her to find any hope.

It wasn't long after her prayer that Ulva found herself in the middle of a dreamy world. She had given up the autonomy of her body. Her limbs had shrunk to almost non-existence. Her body was unable to respond to any feeling. It had gone so stiff that even the slightest shackle was making her fear for her life. Hanging in the middle of nowhere was she, an inanimate object: a locket. The light shining on her glass body was almost blinding her, but the sensations were still stronger. The train was on its way to an unknown destination. For the first few minutes, Ulva didn't make any effort to discover her surroundings.

The train stopped at a station and everyone started leaving their cabins except her owner. Her owner had fallen asleep by then. Ulva finally started her struggle for complete autonomy but all her efforts were in vain. The cabin was getting colder with time. Ulva could see her body resting against a soft sweater. The window was open and a few snowflakes landed near her, while the fog left by them started creeping up her body.

The train left the station and the cabins were once again packed with people of all kinds. Some had already said goodbye to their travel partners, while the others were just joining. Ulva was silently hanging in her place, waiting anxiously for the destination to arrive. After a tiring journey, they reached an unfamiliar station. Ulva's owner entered a garden that was located close to the station. She kept counting her owner's steps during this time, anticipating to see a beautiful destination. The garden had a small wooden cottage in it and the owner lived there all alone.

After entering the cottage, she was left once again hanging near a window. The window was presenting a majestic picture of the backyard. The backyard was home to two bedazzling peacocks and one peahen, and the flowers looked exotic too. The kinds were so mesmerizing that the yard looked like a nook of heaven. Each of the two peacocks and the peahen had unique feathers with intricate patterns. The wonders of the garden were already catching Ulva's attention. The peahen was pregnant. The father of the child was draped in a magnificent white cloak while the other peacock was all black.

However, the beauty of the garden was soon declared to be a blatant lie. The evilness surrounding this mystic beauty was making the place seem like the worst of the places to ever exist. Satan had left his demonic influence here too. Humans believe that Satan just deceives them, but animals too are vulnerable to his attacks. Emotions play a vital role in their world just like ours. Their relations and responsibilities are no different than humans. They get stuck in the very same dilemmas and they too make sacrifices to keep their world in order. In short, Ulva learned one lesson: the universe is a test for everyone and nature doesn't expect perfection from living beings. They have free will and this is what makes them the ones who get questioned for their deeds.

The night started unfolding its secrets, and the moonlight was illuminating the bitter realities of the night. The wolves kept howling and the owls were expecting to witness a barbaric incident. Ulva could already sense the gravity surrounding the place. Everything seemed calm and in-order, but little did everyone know that the events following this cunning calmness would reveal to humanity the worst of the realities: hatred. No category wants to own it because it unleashes the worst form of a being. No one could ever decide whether hatred is a feeling, an emotion, an act of brutality, or an after-effect of suffering.

Every story has its own explanation for this word. However, love is always at war with hatred. Every single being in this world is waiting to declare one of them the ultimate champion. But one thing is known, either of them can make humanity witness the most painful tale.

The peahen was about to lay the eggs resting in her body. These eggs were destined to make everyone learn an important lesson, especially Ulva. All the waking eyes were gazing at the peahen, but to their surprise, she only laid one egg. Everyone understood the decree. The breaths were getting shallower with each increasing second. The tale had been finally officiated and the two peacocks had started fighting each other with utter barbarism. The black peacock attacked the newly become father and heartlessly slit his throat with his talon. The white peacock immediately fell to the ground. While he kept looking around expecting someone to come forward, there was nothing that could be done to prevent his breath from getting diminished. He kept begging for his life but the teary eyes were the only thing that he could gain from his death. The mother of his child was standing in one corner with a lowered head from shame. Her reaction took everyone by surprise as if she too was involved in this. Ulva was seeing this painful scene from the room while the coldness of the surroundings kept penetrating her casing.

The father kept looking at his son for the last few seconds of his life, while his round blood-filled eyes captured the sight of betrayal. When his soul was about to leave his body, everybody could see his beak moving as if he was casting a revenge spell at the garden. The moment he became lifeless, the backyard was taken over by bone-chilling coldness. The peahen kept resting her head on the egg and wept. The owls, the wolves, the flowers, everyone wept but not in solidarity with her, instead, they were looking up to forwarding their condolences to the about-to-be-born kid. Ulva could see her body cracking from the pressing heaviness of her sadness.

Everyone expected the night to end here but little did they know that when Satan decides to inflict someone with his fatal attack, he opts for the most painful way. The eyes of the black peacock were still burning with rage. Everybody could see the black soul emitting negative energies through his eyes. What he was about to do next has never been given any name in the dictionary because of its extremism. The events following the fight made everyone shriek with pain. The peacock started walking slowly towards that infallible being. The mother was unaware of his intentions. His steps were getting heavy as if the earth wanted to stop him from what he was about to do. This was the time when satanic influence triumphed and made everyone lose trust in other living entities.

The peahen was still crying over her vulnerability but Satan, in the shape of a black peacock, was soon going to malign the pure sentiment called *Love.* His plans to hurt its reputation got unveiled that day. The black peacock got closer to the egg and snatched it from the mother. The mother was hit by such a shock that her body got stiff. She tried to lurch forward but the stabbing pain made her hit a boulder.

He moved a little far away from her so he could fulfill his evil desires. He used his sharp talons to invade the lining protecting the innocent being from the shackles of the world, and crushed the child mercilessly to death. The mother shrieked with pain. Her eyes started dripping blood instead of tears. Her feathers started getting dispersed, and she crumpled in front of everyone's eyes. She tried to leap towards her kid but the pain had already inflicted her body with the worst of its effects. Her heart exploded and a sharp light started piercing everyone's vision. The light was so intense that every wailing creature present at that time started turning blind. Ulva could feel too that her sight was getting lost somewhere in between the streets of suffering and endurance. She dropped to the floor after experiencing the pain and shattered into innumerable pieces.

This attempt for theft of breaths wrote its tale, the tale that was going to have a far-reaching impact. The unsuccessful attempt to malign the purest of all relations, love, had become a lesson in itself. The sacrifice of the peahen and the hatred of the peacock made it clear that their love wasn't mutual. The peahen was driven by love while the peacock was driven by hatred. This is why the end of the story was not hopeless. The tale was completed with a lesson that hatred can't be eliminated but it can be fought.

Ulva woke up from heartache. She started sobbing immediately. She grabbed Dwayne's phone. When she opened it, she got to see what she had already been waiting for, the texts from the unknown number.

11

Plankton hadn't met Vernon for quite some time so he decided to pay a sudden visit. By the time he reached the door of the house, Vernon was busy taking a shower so he was unable to open it for a few minutes. Vernon lept towards the door as soon as he got done.

"Sorry, I was taking a shower," said Vernon while gasping.
"Catch your breath and no need to apologize, I can understand," replied Plankton while he followed Vernon to the lounge.
"Wait here while I bring you something to eat."
"No, I am full. Thanks for the hospitality."
"What kind of hospitality, I already owe you quite a lot." Vernon smiled, and his smile was so cheery that it made even Plankton blush. Vernon went to the kitchen to prepare Bolognese pasta.
"I have been practicing this recipe quite a lot these days. I hope the taste has gotten any

better," said Vernon while his head was peeking from the door, "Honestly, it tasted awful the first time." Vernon chuckled.

"It is good that you haven't forgotten to crack jokes. Our future interactions would have been rather dry because I am quite boring."

Plankton laughed with his half-open eyes as tiredness had already started hitting his body. He kept taking deep breaths just to prevent himself from falling asleep at the wrong time.

"Why did you not unlock the door with the key you have? It was cold outside —"
"I never wanted you to know about that key but I had been given it by your dad for emergency purposes. You know very well that your father would need medical aid frequently, so I decided to take matters into my hands. After all, I couldn't let go of any chance to protect my dear friend."

There was silence for a few minutes after what Plankton said, and then Vernon tried to tackle the unwanted seriousness in the room with a different topic.

"I think there can't be any better moment to introduce my beautiful wife." Vernon hadn't called Willa but he was trying to prepare Plankton for the introduction.

There was silence once again in the room.

Plankton's expression had become stern and he looked scared as if he had to confront some reality soon. He looked concerned because he didn't want to make it worse for Vernon. It hadn't been long since he got his last episode. The wounds had recently been healed and Plankton wanted to avoid any unwanted suffering at all costs. He was waiting for Vernon to say something because he wasn't ready to talk himself. He was avoiding the conversation all this time just to prevent himself from blurting out something triggering and hurtful. And then, Vernon left the kitchen to call Willa.

"Willa, look we have a guest," Vernon called her with a gentle voice.

No one entered except the saddening silence that took over the room and the hush that descended upon them. Vernon placed a table in front of Plankton and left the appetizing dish on it, while he went to his room to check on Willa.

"Let me call her. She might be taking a shower." Vernon left Plankton alone with his guilt.

Plankton could hear Vernon calling Willa, and his eyes started getting filled with tears. After a few minutes, Vernon came out of his room with a disappointed look. He rushed towards the guest room while Plankton could see that Vernon had started getting a panic attack. Plankton began to sob while witnessing Vernon dashing into one room and then another. His expressions showed that he was hiding something, some secret or some truth. He was sitting silently while the guilt of staying silent was making his shoulders go heavy. Vernon slipped on the floor and almost hit his head with a pillar. He started wailing like a small child. Plankton left his seat and ran as fast as he could to make Vernon calm down.

> "She was here, I swear she was here. We even talked before I went to take a shower. Trust me!" Vernon wept while his voice kept breaking because of hiccups.

Plankton felt heartbroken seeing Vernon in such a situation. He tried to relax him as much as possible, and after a few moments, Vernon stopped weeping. Plankton took him to the lounge and made him eat something, but a few tears were still rolling down his cheeks and he was unable to eat anything.

After Vernon was ready to hear something, Plankton told him a truth that struck him like lightning. His eyes stayed open for the longest and tears got frozen in them. His body was unable to decide whether it wanted to cry over this news or nullify it. Vernon thought that it was just a judgment by Plankton based on what he had been observing for the past many years, but the strange part was that he wasn't the first person who told him such a thing. Finally, after a lot of thinking, he decided to reply in the harshest way possible, but it wasn't surprising because his whole existence was somehow challenged by Plankton.

"You lie! You are lying just like many others did. You just want to prove that I have gone mad and you all want to send me to a mental asylum." Vernon tried to explain what he thought of Plankton at that time, while he started wailing once again.

"I swear, this isn't what I want. I want you to get better once again. I want you to always—" Plankton was about to complete the sentence when he got interrupted by Vernon, "Just tell me one thing! What kind of revenge are you guys seeking? Do you all want me to die in complete misfortune and utter loneliness?"

"We just want you to stay happy and healthy."

Vernon kept weeping vehemently after listening to the revelation that was somehow canceling his entire existence. There was just one sound that kept making the house the most painful place to exist at that moment, the sound of a heart-breaking whimper. Vernon's eyes were stuck on the ground, while his body seemed to be losing its battle.

After a few minutes of no conversation, Vernon stood up and started walking with heavy steps toward the kitchen. He would stop after every few steps but something was compelling him to keep going. The harsh revelations were what impacted Vernon the most. Vernon went to the kitchen and then came out with a sharp blood-stained knife, and started walking towards Plankton.

Plankton kept following Vernon's steps with his eyes, and by this time his heart had started beating fast. He was scared for his life but equally concerned for Vernon's condition.

"You don't want to do this," said Plankton with a shaky voice.
"I regret that I have to do it just to protect myself from any more suffering." Vernon kept sobbing and his eyes were begging for help as if he was possessed by some demonic energy.

It was getting difficult for Plankton to decide what made the night the most painful for him, seeing his best friend's son in such a dreadful situation or seeing his life flashing before his eyes.

"Don't do this, my dear boy. I will explain everything to you but now is not the right time for this. I know you want this mystery to end, but I promise, you will get to know the matters very soon."
"Willa exists! She bloody exists! I have loved her and I have felt her! Don't you dare to challenge my mental health."
"Nobody is doing it. I just shared what I deemed necessary, and I know it is difficult for you, but I promise that I will make it easy."

Vernon thought about something, closed his eyes, and rushed towards Plankton while pointing the knife at him. Plankton grabbed the vase near him and hit Vernon with it. He fell to the floor. By this time, Plankton had started getting angry at what Vernon opted for.

"I told you, you stupid chap. I told you to wait," Plankton was anguished while he uttered these words for Vernon, "If you actually want to hear the truth then let me tell you. Yes! You are mad! Mad as hell! I hope the news brings you calmness. You were brought to me even when you were young, but I bet you have gone more insane since then," Plankton said this so unhesitantly that he didn't even get time to choose the right words.

These words inflicted pain on Vernon to such an extent that he could feel his heart ripping into God knows how many pieces, and he could see the chunks of his existence falling to the ground. The knife fell from his hand while he got unconscious due to the hitting, and his tears kept seeping into the ridges on the floor.

Plankton was still angry with what Vernon was about to do to him, but after a few minutes, he started feeling guilty for losing his composure. He took Vernon to his room with teary eyes. After waiting for many hours, he lost hope in seeing Vernon awake any sooner. He kept staring at the creases of his palm as if he wanted to extract the hidden revelations that were going to make up his future. While doing so, he saw something scary and clenched his fist tightly.

He turned on the music on the phonograph, brought a clean glass with some water in it, and left it on the table standing near Vernon's bed. He kept looking at it with a heartbroken face. After a few moments, he took out a pouch with crushed pills in it from his pocket and added it to the water. Tears started rolling down his collars, finally dripping on the table, while he dissolved the powder in the water with his trembling fingers. After getting done, he left the house with a wrecked gait and a broken heart.

12

13, February

The final goodbye churned all the emotions associated with sadness and encapsulated pearls in shells lying on a deserted island stretching along their eyelids. The final goodbye to everything, their livelihood, their past, their present, and their expected future in the house (the one that nurtured them to become the new version of themselves) was nothing less than heart-shattering for them. Ulva's steps were faint but this gentleness had some wisdom behind it. She couldn't take her eyes off the things that she had once exhibited in this house. Her foggy breath kept brushing against the edges of the walls, and the mist left by it kept getting crystallized into rigid flakes capturing her last greetings. The house felt as if it was leaning forward to offer a last hug to Ulva. The bristles of her eyelashes were soaking in the warm tears. The only thing that kept Ulva going was the responsibility lying on her shoulders.

Dwayne felt miserable but he had accepted the fact that the ship of his life was finally going to get anchored at an expected shore. He already knew the geographics of the shore and he was happy to finally get a peaceful end. His past was not that ideal, so anything that would somehow get him peace, satisfied him. The wooden floor of the house was curling in as if it wanted Ulva and Dwayne to reconsider the thought of leaving. The goodbye was more difficult than they expected it to be. Their bodies were being subjected to a shaking impact from the sudden burst of memories.

The silent goodbyes were finally over, and now, both of them got hit by another bitter and painful reality, the reality that both of them were never going to meet each other again. Although there had been no exchange of words between them, their eyes had been continuously conversing this whole time. Both of them finally realized that their destinations were lying at opposite ends. Somehow they got so engrossed in the thought of fulfilling the rites lying on their ends that they didn't even get the time to enjoy the presence of each other. The realization was slowly hitting them and they decided to say the final goodbye to each other.

Regardless of knowing the painful reality that two

lovers were going to separate, neither of them uttered even a single word. The gentle kiss served as the final goodbye for them. Both the souls felt a tremble when they started walking toward opposite ends of the road. The sky was witnessing the divine decree, a decree that was soon going to remove the veil from the casket of untold truths. It had been already taken out from the burial, but now was the time when the tale was going to reveal the hidden secrets sewn to it. The birds remained hiding in the trees that day and nobody dared to get even slightly involved in these enigmatic events.

Finally, Dwayne was en route to his gothic village. He had never dared to return to his village since the day he got married to Ulva, but as his struggle to live happily with her had entered an endless dark lane, he decided to risk his existence just for the sake of getting some peace. He decided to participate in *Atak*, a sacrificial satanic ritual. He was aware of the odds of him surviving because the festival was believed to get invaded by unworldly creatures every time. He was ready to put his life at stake even if he had to wait for death till the last drop of blood oozed out of his body.

He finally reached his destination. Now, he had to reach the epicenter of the mystic forest. His brain was becoming numb. The aroma was strange and the air was suffocating him. It was getting darker and the star 'Sigil of Baphomet', chalked with the crushed bones of owls in the center of the forest, was eventually getting filled with more and more people. The leaves of the trees in the forest had a leathery texture. The area was getting hotter. One could expect the land to be stretched on the top of hell. Dwayne was already convinced that there was some demonic presence that was making the place frightening.

The wilting flowers had sharp needles. The needles were piercing the ovaries of the flowers, but the strange part was that blood was getting filled into the wilted cups. The ovaries looked like that of any human. They were stirring a pungent smell in the atmosphere, making it even more unbearable to breathe. Dwayne was turning white because nothing felt right. He had already signed up to participate in the ritual and there was no option for him to back out. He had started missing Ulva, but his ugly present compelled him to stay focused on his surroundings.

The sigil got jam-packed with everyone, and then they all waited for their supreme. Each one of them was carrying a worn-out sack. The place was smelling rotten as if a heap of dead bodies was lying close to the sigil. Dwayne's body started stiffening because the fear creeping into his heart kept mutilating his soul. His eyes were filled with tears but he was trying his best to hold them back. All the good memories began to flash before his eyes. He could sense the angel of death to be wandering around.

The lamps were finally lit because the supreme had arrived. Hush descended on the large crowd. Dwayne was trying to keep his head down to avoid catching anyone's attention. His chest was putting strain on his heart and he had started hyperventilating. His eyes were getting smaller due to terror. The supreme began to address the gathering while standing on an elevated platform erected at the center of the sigil. The star's pointed ends were connected by chalking a circle to prevent the interference of unwanted creatures.

After a few moments, the ritual was officiated. Everyone opened the sacks they were holding. The supreme was standing on the platform with his sack. It was hanging right at the top of Dwayne's head. His head started feeling something moist dripping at it, and then it started running down his forehead. When Dwayne rubbed his finger on his forehead to see it, he immediately screamed and started panicking. It was human blood. By now, all the myths that he had heard before, were turning out true. Dwayne started looking around eagerly. He could see human corpses everywhere. He was disgusted and horrified. It was getting difficult for him to breathe. He passed out within a few minutes. The people surrounding him kept doing their work and nobody bothered to check on him.

Everybody was occupied in the process of cutting open the corpses. The place was soon echoing with the sound of cracking bones. The attitude of the attendees towards the bodies seemed revengeful. They were taking delight in the petrifying process. Soon, Dwayne gained consciousness back. The blood was still dripping on his body. He was feeling miserable for serving the evil desires of Satan. He dared to ask someone about the bodies and the reply was even more gut-wrenching. He was told that these bodies were of their enemies, and they were doing this out of hatred to amuse themselves and Satan.

Dwayne kept vomiting while the people were busy mutilating the corpses. The sharp cracking sounds were soon taken over by squeaky sounds. All of them were busy pulling out the organs from the bodies. The star was filled with chunks of flesh and the maggots had already started crawling in them. A clot of blood plopped out and fell on Dwayne's shoe. A tear fell from his left eye spontaneously. He tried his best to keep his body in control because he knew it well that a fuss maker would meet a dreadful end in such a place. The organs were slipping and falling around him while he had his eyes shut.

Against his expectations, the festivities weren't over yet. The organs were already discarded, and now the boundary was circling empty dead bodies.

Dwayne was standing close to a body while its pelvic bone was brushing against his leg. He was unable to push it away. The dreadful night had started revealing some of its evilest secrets. Dwayne's heart was in terrible agony.

Soon, the place started getting lit with the luminous reflections cast by the sharp knives. Everyone was holding them against the throats of innocent and harmless animals, and on the call of the supreme, they slit the throats barbarically. Dwayne could see the spilling blood forming a fountain around the sigil, while his heart was shattering from dismay. This ritual presented a scene that was enough to invoke the end of time. He kept cursing Satan for his utterly barbaric lust for suffering, who was doing this just to declare hatred as the triumphed one. Dwayne could feel the heat from hell wrenching the wrinkles of demonic entities present around him.

Brutality had no limit that day. The animals were beheaded, mutilated, and their organs were removed. Satan kept extending the limits of his atrocities. The rituals were being carried out effortlessly. Dwayne was hoping that God's wrath would uproot this filthy piece of land and dump it in hell, but the night was bereft of any divine presence. The organs removed from the bodies of the brutally silenced animals were stuffed into the human corpses. The animals were getting wrongfully involved for satanic objectives.

The behavior didn't look revengeful to Dwayne, instead, it seemed as if it was the evil desire to become outrageously heinous that was making them do this.

After they were done stuffing the bodies, they started stitching their skin back. The bodies still seemed empty. No curse worked that day to end the events from unraveling any further. The anticipation in the air kept growing with time, and now, multiple bodies were lying around, while their stomachs could be seen bloating with the impure potions pumped down their throats. The place soon started echoing with chants and hails to summon Satan. Nothing seemed working and Satan didn't show up. The disappointed entities started gathering coals and set the trees on fire. The place felt like a burning bowl, boiling everyone present in the vicinity. Dwayne started coughing from the ashes rising into the air, while the added heat kept stifling him.

However, his sensations soon began to diminish after seeing the most soul-wrenching and mind-freezing ritual of the day. The bodies were thrown into the blinding blaze. The corpses started to explode because of the potions filled in them, and the ashes started falling like snowflakes. The rotten smell generated was unbearable. Everybody cheered while twirling in the shower of ashes. Dwayne once again burst into tears. He knew that this was the last time he was going to cry, so he shrieked as loud as he could to make everyone aware of the pain he was suffering from.

Finally, the divine wrath arrived and the blazes started getting anguished, as if they were representing God's anger. The place got completely chaotic and everybody started running from fear of death, but Dwayne was calm as if he was ready for the wrath to take him in its influence. He started reminiscing about his good memories for one last time. Satan's followers kept hollering, but their attempts to save themselves from the wrath were of no help. The fire had started transgressing the sigil's boundaries, ultimately burning everyone.

Everybody burned down to ashes, and the hollering sounds started getting fainter. That night, God revealed one of the decrees from the casket of untold truths. Satan didn't appear but he got to see his defeat. This was one of the numerous attempts that he had made to defend his ally: hatred.

Ulva was in the middle of her journey when she suddenly felt chills running down her spine. Little did she know that she lost the companion whom she had vowed to stay with till her death.

13

The floor felt a tremble. The bed kept getting impacted by the jolts. The glass filled with water on his side table fell on the floor and shattered into many pieces. It spilled its content on the floor, and the evil intentions of Satan got revealed once again. The wooden floor started to generate a mist that traveled up to the roof, and then condensed into a black deposition that made Vernon witness the extent of Divine protection. The earthquake revealed the hidden divine decree.

The migraine caused Vernon to wake up in complete bewilderment. His eyes had become smaller, and the pain was spreading all around his back. The pain was so intense that it slowly started numbing his sensations. His vision was getting blurry, his ears felt like a shelter to some buzzing creatures, and his sinuses were blocked thus intensifying the pain caused by migraine. When he swung his arm to grab the glass of water, he discovered the broken pieces of glass sparkling like jewels from the beam of light falling upon them. He kept trying to make his senses accommodate him in combating this suffering, but nothing seemed to be working for him. His mouth was so dry that he could feel the reserves of his saliva to be bereft of all the moisture. His tongue kept sticking to the walls of his mouth. He tried to stand up but his body was unable to keep his movement coordinated. The back of his head was still sore from the attack, thus influencing the numbing of his senses.

After a few minutes, he started to get hold of his consciousness completely except for his sensations. He started to remember the conversation he had with Plankton. The ugly confessions had begun making him uneasy once again. His heart felt wounded as if it was stabbed with a poisoned dagger. The words started echoing within his head and chest, and kept piercing every organ resting within their enclosed walls. He was unable to stop the trail of tears from seeping into the newly formed wounds. He kept questioning God for the reason for such magnitude of difficulties making his life miserable. He felt heartbroken over the betrayals that he had faced in his life. He could feel the fierce waves taking away his identity. He started thinking about his complicated past. By now, it was getting difficult for him to classify it as a good or bad one.

Whenever he would try to think of the beautiful memories that he had made with Stephen and all his loved ones, his mind would start taking in the hurtful memories from the channel of his ugly past. The library holding the books of predestination and decree for everyone on earth had started witnessing cracks in its shelves. Only God knew the wisdom hidden behind these sacrifices.

Satan had started a barbaric war and to tackle his barbarism, a painful combat strategy was needed, and nature had revealed it already on Vernon that he was one of the chosen representatives. Even Vernon was trying to accept the wisdom hidden behind his painful struggle, but the magnitude of pain was making it almost unbearable for him to accept this as his fate. The never-stopping tears escaping his eyes were making his body more destitute each day. He wanted to die already, but it couldn't be fathomed that who he was waiting for this whole time.

However, a part of him had somehow understood his responsibility too, and was trying to get this tale a hopeful ending. It was evident that the end wouldn't get any easier for him, but the significant lesson left behind by him was going to get written in the books, so he had to act accordingly. He knew that there were going to be more Vernons in the future, and for them, he had to leave a lesson of ultimate strength.

Vernon kept falling asleep after every few moments. He would wake up with the hope to meet someone who would help him out. He knew that God was his sole companion in this struggle, but he was in dire need of a helping hand from a human. Finally, after a few hours, his senses started to get back to normal. Although he tottered, he managed to reach his fridge to grab some food. He gulped the water and quenched his thirst. The complete autonomy of his body started to grant him some serenity. He would try to stop himself from crying, but would miserably fail in his attempts.

After getting himself some break from the aftereffects of misery, he went back to his bed and fell asleep. This time, he slept like some small kid who had no worries in his life. He slept so peacefully that even the surroundings silenced themselves to avoid any interruption in the process of the resurrection of his broken soul. For a few moments, it seemed as if he was getting his liveliness back. He didn't seem bereft of eternal peace anymore. But it didn't last long, because the light of hope started to diminish after a few hours. His body started to suffer from the agony of revenge once again. He started sweating profusely, while his eyes were still shut. The restlessness stayed with him for a few moments, and then he opened his eyes wide as if his body had pledged to never sleep again. When he started to get aware of his surroundings once again, he found Willa sleeping on the opposite side of the bed. Her face was facing the door. She looked tired because her hands were pulling her legs towards her chest. Her fatigued body was making her bones feel weak.

By now, Vernon was getting terrified of Willa's habitual sudden reappearances. She would get lost somewhere in the house (almost to non-existence), but after some hours, she would reappear and her coming back would startle Vernon. He started panicking in the bed and moved to one corner of it. His heart was pounding with great force. His skin started getting paler because of the stupefaction. He was scared to go near Willa, waking her up was the last thing that he could think of. It was painful for him to witness that his lover of many years had turned his life into a nightmare. He was horrified by the idea of coexisting with a betrayer like her. He had started getting disgusted by her presence. Vernon thought that half of his worries were caused by her. He used to look for the missing pieces of his broken heart in her, but now, he wanted her to die. That selfless sentiment for her wouldn't ooze out of him anymore.

He wanted this night to lead his relationship with Willa to a decisive end. He had started thinking of possible ideas to get rid of her. He didn't care about her condition anymore. He believed that she was up to something dangerous, and that she had been planning about making his life even more miserable. He had lost respect for her. The marsupium that was home to the intense feelings that he had for her, had been torn open long ago. He was assured by her antics that she was a representative sent by Satan, and that she was there to weaken him spiritually, but the plans of God had revealed the truth.

They entered into the midnight phase, the phase when many lovers look at the moon and trace the cracks that are visible to their eyes. Vernon plunged into the sea of recollection. It is believed that Satan cries too when he looks at the bright moon. He cries over his fate, but later, he vows to invade the universe with his demonic desires. His desires make the wolves howl as they swear their allegiance to him. The bats cover their ears to hinder penetration by the sound of chants from hell. The owls keep their eyes wide open and cast counter spells to pierce the cloak of evilness that tries to take over the universe.

Vernon grabbed the knife lying in the lounge and started approaching the bed. Willa was sleeping peacefully. The moonlight was getting reflected from the shining edges, and was finally illuminating Vernon's broken heart. He could think of no other option but to kill Willa. He kept walking steadily and quietly. When he reached near her, he stopped for a moment. He took a long breath, while his tears kept rolling down his sunken cheeks. He raised his arms above his head and attacked her. He kept stabbing her until he was sure that she was dead.

The knife kept puncturing her heart while Vernon cried at his misery. The knife continued stabbing her body but no blood escaped the delicate walls of her chest. In fact, Vernon's vision started getting diminished. The only thing that he could see in front of his eyes were some unidentifiable patterns. He would hear a buzzing sound in his ears whenever he would shove his knife-holding hand down Willa's ribs. He attacked her without even the slightest resistance, and this kept boggling him. However, the patterns started to transform into new ones and eventually blinded his eyes completely.

Vernon stumbled and started falling on everything present in his vicinity. The sounds started growing louder for him, while the house started echoing with the sounds of cracking furniture and shattering glass. He started panting. Suddenly, he heard a noise as if someone had entered his house. He was unable to see the intruder. He kept staggering across the room when he suddenly felt a needle pricking his neck. He immediately fell to the ground and passed out.

14

13, February

She draped herself in the wool shawl, an old gift from Dwayne. The cold weather was worsening her asthma. Her bones were aching from the intense shivering. The accumulating fatigue had started affecting her muscle coordination. She was making use of rigid supports around her to keep her going. She kept taking deep breaths because even the shortest walk was putting a strain on her chest. She was trying to delay the time of her departure as she simply couldn't say goodbye to the city that was her home for the past decade.

The land still looked barren. The curse hadn't been lifted yet. Ulva was appalled to embark on a journey that had a bed of thorns laid along the way. She was concerned about the consequences. She wasn't ready to witness the end of this tale, although she didn't want to look back too. She just wanted things to get back to normal, but little did she know that a war spurred by Satan always has a sacrificial ending.

The roses were wilting and their petals were curling, as if they wanted to lessen their exposure to the darker times. The sun looked deprived of its loftiness and splendor. The colors reflecting from the silver lining of the clouds were getting overshadowed by the gloomy shades. The sky looked like home to no other creature but vultures.

The bus was ready to leave for Onerwaarten. Ulva had fallen asleep, but the sudden loud announcement startled her. She was unable to stand straight, but another woman held her by her arms and assisted her to the ticket counter. Her body was suffering from a terrible fever and could be seen to be bending downwards. Her dark circles were making her squinting eyes look smaller.

The woman helping Ulva didn't dare to ask her about her past, because the fear of her dying from the eminent pain compelled her to ignore the details. Ulva's tiredness was evident from the fact that she fell asleep the moment she sat in her seat. The seat was doing its job quite well by keeping together the pieces of her body, as they could fall apart with any jolt. After a few moments, she started snoring. The snores were loud but nobody seemed to get bothered, because the chatters on the bus were louder. The bus started its journey. Nothing could disturb Ulva's sleep as she stayed unaffected by her surroundings. She was dreaming about Dwayne. The dream wasn't dreamy at all because it was the literal depiction of her thoughts. The untold truths that never got revealed to Dwayne constituted her major worries. Even the journey wouldn't be this much difficult if she hadn't witnessed such an abrupt end with Dwayne. The unexpressed feelings were making her worries feel even more distressing.

As the bus started getting closer to Onerwaarten, the magnitude of Ulva's restlessness kept increasing. She had started panicking. The journey had finally entered the portal withholding the final spells. The next few days were going to be the decisive ones for this conflict between love and hatred. Everyone had started preparing themselves to witness the unimaginable end of barbarism and heartbreak. When the bus was around 20 km away from the destination, her restlessness reached to an extent that her eyes popped open and she sat in her seat immediately. The stunned look in her eyes concerned the woman sitting next to her. She tried her best to calm Ulva after seeing her suffering from the imminent misery.

They finally reached the infamous city. The weather was drier than Verrot. The animals surrounding the bus stand looked petrified. The cats seemed hungry, while the dogs were thirsty.

They kept circling the bus as if they were waiting for a guest. Everyone left the bus except Ulva. She was breathing heavily, and the anxiety was proving to be fatal for her already wrecked body. She kept sighing from the intense pain that was wrenching her whole body. She grabbed her purse and descended the stairs of the bus. The moment her heels touched the land, something made her stumble. She tottered for the rest of her journey as if the land wasn't ready to accept her presence.

She settled herself on the bench placed near the bus stand. Suddenly a thought hit her and she realized that her luggage was missing. The two bags were nowhere to be seen. The driver and the workers kept searching for them but all to no avail. Ulva already started sobbing. Her cold and trembling hands covered her mouth while she cried from dismay. Plus the thought of Dwayne being in a difficult situation was aggravating her worries, and worsening her pain. She could feel that Dwayne was confronting the last spells of his fate. She sat on the bench and kept weeping. The driver and the workers gave up and went back to their work. The piercing cold kept stinging her body. She called Dwayne multiple times but got no response. She was cursing herself for not thinking of calling him before because now, it had gotten too late. She was convinced that her fate wasn't going to show her any mercy in the future too.

She stopped a cab and embarked upon her final

journey. The driver's appearance kept bothering her. He was covering his face, while the oversized cap kept falling on his shoulder. His baggy clothes hid his obese weight quite well. He was stinking as if he was drunk. Ulva was concerned about him driving the car in such a condition, but later, she didn't seem to notice much because her olfactory receptors got used to the smell. The seats of the cab were worn out. The springs in the seats were visible and Ulva kept getting uneasy. The journey from the bus stand was going to take her one more hour.

She hadn't opened her purse since she had left Verrot. She was feeling hungry so she decided to look for any food item in it. She found a bar of chocolate but something strange caught her attention. She found a crumpled paper. She took it out and when she discovered the sentiments penned on it, she started shedding tears once again. She recognized the writing; it was Dwayne's final goodbye. She placed the letter on her heart, while her right hand covered her mouth to silence her miserable shriek. She embraced the letter for a few minutes and then started reading it.

My sweetheart,

I know this time is quite difficult for you. I know that you must be thinking of giving

up, but let me tell you, I have never seen a strong human like you in my life. I have been seeing you suffering for many years, but your resilience always inspired me. No doubt whatever happened to you, you never thought of giving up, and nor should you now. I know that you are tired of misery invading your peace, but don't you remember the noble cause that you have been chosen for? Don't tell me that you haven't realized the fact that you are the CHOSEN ONE. You have to leave behind a lesson for millions. Many Ulvas are looking forward to you, so tell them your story. You have been very brave, trust me! Don't let these mild waves take away your determination. My spirit of endurance disappeared quite a while ago, so I ultimately decided to give up. I was never a strong fella. We losers need to learn something from people like you. I am proud of you. Put this war to a temporary end and make the sentiments of love triumph. I will be watching over you, and I know that you will leave behind a huge impact.

We didn't get to talk before departing, but let me justify my silence. I was ashamed. Yes, I lost the ability to articulate my thoughts the day I found out about our son. The sacrifices that you had made in the past really put me to shame. It was late for me to go back and make things normal. I had been blinded by hatred for all these years, and had already sworn my allegiance to the Satan-led cause, so I couldn't find a way out. I had no right to question you about your decisions and decided to stay silent. There was nothing left to talk about. I was lost somewhere in the dungeons of hopelessness, while Satan chained me and there was no other way to escape it except ending my life. I am not ashamed of giving up my existence because I was not a good person. I have done horrible stuff in my life and I deserve to get punished. I know this isn't a justification at all, but I was blinded by your love. Lately, I had started punishing myself for the countless sins that I had committed in my life. I am so sorry that I wasn't kind to you in the last few days, it was just that I didn't want you to suffer with me by getting involved. I was the one who deserved to get convicted for the gut-wrenching sins I had committed, so I wanted to keep you away from me. I am sorry but I just wanted you to hate me, because I knew that my death wouldn't get any easier for you.

I never got to tell you this but I loved you even before you met Erasmus. I would be unable to keep my heart in control whenever I would see you, and eventually, I was smitten with you. Your beauty had no match, and it would make it more difficult for me to ignore your presence. My working days would feel dry without you, as I used to look forward to meeting you at the pharmacy. I was always convinced that the aura you retained was a divinely granted gift. I could never accept you with Erasmus and my jealousy took everyone in its wrath. It made me do many horrible things and killing Erasmus was one of them.

I don't know whether my son will forgive me for murdering his Godfather, as I don't deserve to get forgiven. I hated my son, what could get worse than that? I falsely claim to be ridden by love, it was my hatred that made me commit such horrible sins. My hatred made many others lose their innocence, Garth was one of them. I made him gulp the bitter potion of greed and I will get punished for this too. I feel disgusted to my core that I got that poor boy a dreadful end. I gave Garth the hope that I would make him marry the love of his life if he would poison Erasmus for me. Do you see it? I misused every other pure sentiment: hope, love, care, and trust. I used them unjustly and for my gain.

I must have been the strongest ally of Satan. I unwantedly made him an apparent victor in this war. But the offense that broke me the most was breaking your trust.

I am going to participate in a Satanic ritual and the chances of me surviving are negligible. I have already made you the owner of my property, I hope it's enough to fund you and my beloved son. Please try to make him stop hating me because

it will get unbearable for me in the afterworld. I want you to take care of yourself and my son. I will be missing you guys, but I have lived more than I deserve so it's time to say goodbye to this temporary world. I hope we get to meet in the hereafter. I will be waiting for you.

**With love,
Dwayne Steven**

Ulva burst into tears, and there was nothing that could make her weep silently. The quiver was so loud that the cab driver stopped for a moment. Ulva kissed the heartfelt letter written by the love of her life. She didn't seem to care about the ugly and shocking confessions in it. The words started getting washed away with her tears running down the paper, taking with them the heartbreaking sentiments. Her journey finally entered the infinite loop of regret, while her miseries kept her wounds bleeding.

15

Everything felt awake that day. Figuratively, the sun was gloomy, but an apparent eye could see an intensely shining ball of fire blinding everyone. The clouds were trying to get themselves some spot in the sky, as they wanted to offer their final goodbye. The trees looked lifeless, but the abrupt rounds made by the wind were revealing their attentiveness. The colors were fading away, but before departing to the chambers of lifelessness, they wanted to say their final goodbye too. The moist smell brought a message from the forthcoming showers that were expected to wash away the blood. The streets were preparing themselves to provide a rigid pavement to the streaming blood. However, the birds kept hiding in their nests, preventing their kids from looking at the expected end of this deadly tale. The twitters were no longer there. Everybody could just hear the roars of the blowing wind. The sky soon got taken over by the committee of vultures.

They kept whirling around as if they were waiting for a heart-wrenching blood spill.

It soon started raining, but the showers didn't last long. They just cleaned the lanes, and washed away all the impurities and the blackness smudged by Satan's mischievous workers. The moist smell served its role by granting the city's visitors some sense of introspection. The sky already donned the black veil because it was ready to mourn over someone's loss. The atmosphere felt heavy with heavenly presences. It could have been the angels that were there to welcome an upcoming departed soul.

This was another day of Vernon waking in utter bewilderment. He had started getting weaker day by day. One of his ears had already given up the ability to hear because of the blood clotting in its canal. His pillow had found refuge in a red cover knitted by his blood, and its color was so bright that even nature was left bedazzled. His head had gotten tilted towards his left shoulder. The muscles in his neck region were becoming numb with each growing day. It was getting difficult for him to sit straight.

He had completely forgotten the details of last night. Even the blood he saw spilled around him, took him with shock and he immediately tried to rush toward his washroom out of disgust, but his body was too weak to make him do that. He had forgotten his worries for a few moments. He had even forgotten about the intruder breaking into his house and injecting him with some substance. He looked unaware of the significance of the day. He didn't seem to notice much of his surroundings, because the stabbing pain in his body was unbearable to an extent that it wouldn't let him think about anything else.

The sky was still being ruled by dark clouds, but the showers had already stopped. The streets were looking perfectly washed. Everyone had already taken turns saying goodbye to him. Vernon was still under the influence of the medication that was making him feel nauseous, while making his head hurt too. Suddenly the room started smelling strange as if a cadaver was abandoned in its premises. Vernon couldn't smell it properly but the pungent odor still made its way to his nose, sedating his senses even more. It was difficult for him to look around because of his stiff neck, but he still managed to figure out its possible source. When he turned to his right, he got so panic-stricken that his body started shivering violently. He screamed so loud that even the glassware had to get hold of themselves, and the frequency of the shriek was peaking to an extent that he had to cover his own ears. The seizure inflicting his body started getting more and more intense, and he eventually fell to the ground.

Maggots could be seen crawling out of Willa's

mouth. Her forehead had a noticeable bulge, and her eyes had sunken deep into the sockets. The condition of her body could make anyone shriek with fear. Her arms were swelling. Her nails looked smashed, as one could see the remaining bits of her nail plates piercing the nail beds. Blood had dried at the base of her nose. Her stomach looked bloated. Her body had turned fluid-like as if all the bones in her body had been completely crushed. The interior of her chest was visible. The body itself was in such a dreadful condition that one would assume it to be torn open by some hungry beast. The flesh had almost gotten detached from the bones, and the chunks were hanging out of her body. The blood could be seen to have settled in the edges of her cracked bones. Vernon screamed from intense pain when he saw Willa's punctured lungs. The scene was a blood-freezing one for humanity to witness. Vernon gently brushed his hand against her chest, but the thought of touching her rotting flesh made him cry vehemently.

Vernon's intense wails saddened all the things in his surroundings. The heartbreak was real. It was getting difficult for him to comprehend the thought of Willa lying dead. Although he had forgotten that it was he who had attacked her, and that the wounds left by him were what proved fatal. The delusional effects clouding his mind didn't seem lasting long. It was just that he was just hooked with the moment when he had expressed his feelings for her. For a while, his mental state had made him forget his hatred for her. It was the sedation that had put his short-term memory at rest.

The agonizing pain of heartbreak started wrenching his soul once again. His mouth was getting dry. He lunged toward the glass on the side table. He drank the water as if his mouth had gotten dry as dust. He gulped it so fastly that he didn't even check the contents in the glass. The water was turning black as if it was poured from a rusty reserve. The moment he drank it completely, his nose started bleeding. He started to lose consciousness but the dizziness went away after a few minutes.

He hid in a corner. He gasped for air while his body kept trembling from fear. It was not evident whether he was scared for his life, or was it the thought of Willa's heartbreaking departure that impacted him so much. He kept sobbing for many minutes, while his body started to surrender to the wildness of his surroundings. It was getting cold in the room. His clothes were torn and drenched in bodily fluids. He was stinking because of the dirt settling on his body, but the smell of a rotting body was making it worse. He saw the blood stains on his arms, and the thought of coming in contact with a mutilated body made him vomit profusely, and he emptied his bowels. After that, he started vomiting blood. The intensity of shivering took such a pace that Vernon's spine started pounding against the freezing walls, and the blood from his back kept staining the rigid surfaces it was coming in contact with.

Vernon slept on the floor for an hour. He immediately sat down after waking and clenched his fist, as if he wanted to ward off a potential threat by fighting. Maybe he was scared of his dreadful present and wanted to confront it. By now, he was sweating excessively once again, although the coldness had started peaking at this point. He was no longer crying, but the devastation was evident from the uneven steps that he started taking.

He walked toward the lounge because the sun was setting and he wanted to see it. He gazed at the window with his stunned eyes as if this was the last sunset of his life. He immediately fell to the floor close to the couch. He dragged himself with injured hands towards a support and leaned against it. He spread his legs and kept staring at the panes of the window like a curious kid. The tears were still frozen in his eyes, but they needed a vent. He had no energy left to shed more tears, so this time, his soul started getting restless instead. The sun wasn't fully visible as the black clouds wanted to deprive Vernon of this sight, but he was still determined to grant himself a few moments of relish. He wrapped his arms around his legs and placed his chin on his knee.

It had already gotten dark. He was still leaning against the couch, but he wasn't ready to say goodbye to the day. He wanted to engross himself with some more wonders of nature, but the darkness of the day wasn't ready to get him what he wanted. He soon realized that the negative energies were getting much more stubborn so he decided to go back to his room. He couldn't walk properly, so he kept using his hands to support his body whenever it would collapse.

He thought about something for a few seconds, and then approached the phonograph lying on the floor. He corrected its position and played his favorite song on it. The music reel kept working fine for a few minutes. Vernon managed to stand on his bare feet and started making his body dance in sync with the rhythm of the music. He knew the song very well, so it wasn't difficult for him to choreograph his dance. He kept dancing his heart out. He did it until he forgot about his worries and weaknesses. He would fall after every few minutes, but no pain could stop him from dancing at that moment. He was immensely lost in the imaginary world created by the music. He kept swinging his arms in the air out of excitement. He kept laughing while dancing. The innocent laugh was echoing in the house. His knees had started bleeding because of the sudden falls, but he was carefree as if he could feel nothing.

The music turned off itself, and then the phonograph started generating a squeaky noise. Vernon didn't seem to notice and he kept dancing like an innocent child. The noise could make anyone's ears bleed, but a protective cloak was granting Vernon a few more moments of relish. He kept shaking his head while his arms were fully extended in the air, and kept twirling. Surprisingly, he had stopped falling by now.

Suddenly, someone rang the bell. Vernon didn't hear anything. He was busy dancing his heart out. No ballet dancer could have done any better than him. The ringing stopped after a few minutes. The squeaky noise kept bothering everyone in the surroundings except Vernon, but nobody complained while seeing the poor boy being content with whatever he was doing. But something stopped him; he saw a pool of blood touching his bare feet. He didn't give it much attention and started twirling once again. Now, the shrilling sounds had a new partner, the sounds of splashing blood. Vernon's feet kept thumping against the floor, while the drops of blood kept staining his pants. He could hear the splashes too but he didn't want to stop. In fact, the sound of splashing blood could only be heard by him.

The bell stopped ringing for a few moments, but they were followed by gentle knocks on the door. The knocks were so faint that anybody would have assumed the expected guest to be a small kid. The knocks got silenced too after a few minutes. Vernon ended his dance by throwing himself onto the floor. He hit his head but this time, no pain seemed to bother him. He had heard the last few knocks so he was aware of the fact that there was someone on the door. He mustered up the courage to greet his new guest. He kept using his hands to drag himself up till the door, as his energy had once again dwindled to zero. After many efforts, he reached the door. He used the support of the locked door knob to stand up once again. After a few failed attempts, he managed to stand straight and decided to open the door.

16

14, February

Her shoes were half sunk in the mud, and some muddy spots had already formed a crusty layer around her ankles. She was completely drenched with rainwater. Her hair was disoriented, and her mascara had smudged around her cheeks while flowing through the folds of her wrinkled skin. Her breaths were getting shallower with each growing minute. The bench she was sitting on was located at a corner of the park. The lush green grass was hiding under the dirty blanket woven by nature's tears, as if it didn't want anyone to steal it of the fresh colors it was bearing. Ulva was unaware of her surroundings while resting on the wooden bench. The legs of the bench had already been half eaten by termites. The place looked deprived of any sort of human contact.

A gentle breeze interrupted Ulva's few moments

of peace and she opened her eyes immediately. Her eyes were sparkling for no eminent reason. Her eyelids had protruded so much that they were holding all the tears for a while until they reached their limit, and the never stopping trail of crystal-clear tears started streaming down her cheeks. She discovered a shivering cat sleeping next to her on the bench. She removed her scarf and adjusted it gently on the cat's body. Then she took a deep breath and looked at the sky. The sky looked empty. There were no birds at all. No one would have guessed if it weren't for the puddles, that it had rained a few moments ago. Ulva kept searching with her sunken eyes for many things in her surroundings, and it seemed that she had an imaginary checklist of the place in her mind. The look on her face clearly showed that she was comparing the current condition of this place to the one she remembered.

She attempted to stand up thrice, but some unconceivable force was making her drop back into the bench. Her shoes were completely covered with mud because of the weight she was putting on her trembling and weak legs. The place was so silent that her wheezy breath could be heard rattling her fragile ribs. Then a sudden jolt made her fall from the bench onto the ground. By now, her entire clothes had gotten muddy. She didn't seem bothered, instead, she moved forward to grab the arm of the bench. The thin and fragile wooden arm was successful in pulling her body, and she stood up on her fatigued legs.

She started walking towards the gate of the park. She was walking slower than the army of ants marching near her, collecting their final stock for winter. After leaving the park, she looked back once again to catch sight of as many things in the area as possible. She was doing this as if she was determined that her departure from this temporary world was a few breaths away. She moved her right arm towards the squeaky and rusted gate, to use it as a support for her leaning back. After doing so, she burst into tears once again and this time it was a deafening and heartbreaking cry. She kept tossing her head around for a while out of despair as if everything had ended for her. She could see no way out of this. She wanted a divine sign to show her a way, but the world looked too deprived of foreign interventions that day. Nobody wanted to interrupt the flow of events, as her fate was already meeting its destined end. Lessons had to be drawn, and this was how it had to go particularly on that day.

After staying at the same spot for a moment or two, she started her final walk along the sidewalks. The streets were empty. There was no sign of life that day. Everybody knew that the angel of death could be wandering in these streets, and nobody had even the slightest plan to come across him. But Ulva was fearless as she had no fear of losing this so-called gift: Life. The reason for her fearlessness was that she had already pulled this far. She had already concluded her duty of completing the story by jolting it down with the fresh blood pouring out of her aching heart.

She took a turn to a place while being determined that it would be still there: the house of the old woman living next to the city's central park. Ulva wanted to check on her, or maybe offer her final salutations. She considered that woman to be the epitome of many life-changing lessons, and any last-minute advice wouldn't do much damage as things were already settling in their rightful places. When Ulva reached the location, she was left heartbroken once again to find out that the place had a big lock on the door. She considered this a Divine message that nothing is permanent as it seems.

Although the place was shut, she found a small flower shop near it. The smell was already lingering in the proximity of the shop. Ulva decided to enter. An old man was selling many vibrant flowers, while he himself looked very dull and pale. Ulva bought white lilies and paid the man with some extra money. The flowers looked fresh and the smell was making the surrounding quite serene. Now, she had to stop at one more monument of this tale.

The moment she left the shop, a shocking and

disturbing sight caught her attention. The flowers had wilted. The smell had become more rotten and pungent. The petals had already settled deep down in the plastic wrapping of the bouquet. Ulva decided to keep it anyway, and started walking to the last of her stops. She walked for at least 15 minutes before she reached a wrecked place. She stood at some distance from it the moment she caught its glance. Her eyes immediately started looking for support, as she was too weak to bear the burden exerted by the memories creeping around that place. She started sobbing once again, and half of her body had already gotten exhausted of energy to keep her standing straight. Her left hand kept covering her mouth to stop her squeals from echoing in the street. Her eyes and skin had started getting pale.

The rusty and half-broken board of the pharmacy was dangling in the air. It still read 'Fir Jiddereen Pharmacy'. The glass panes were broken. A phenolic smell kept escaping the broken spots. The door of the pharmacy was labeled with barricade tape. When Ulva decided to look inside, a sudden and unavoidable force pushed her back, and the only thing she could see was a dark passage bearing countless memories. She couldn't withstand the sight anymore and left the place without even a single thought.

She was panting and weeping while she left the area. The streets, the city itself, and the unavoidable recollection of memories were killing her, by slowly poisoning her already wrecked body. She started walking to the final destination which was going to be paramount for this tale. The war had entered its final spell and the air had already started getting dense with a suspenseful hue. The heartbeats too had gotten faint for everyone witnessing that night. The night had unusually started to get very cold. The moon looked gloomy, but it was there to say its final goodbye to the expected departing soul.

Everything was coming to an end. Satan was spectating each of the moments from his throne, after all, this war was started by him the moment he was thrown out of the divine court. He was always against love, and then it can be any form of love, brethren love, romantic love, or motherly love. Love had always been poison for him. He wanted to prove in this story that love was always destined to lose, but little did he know that death is not a loss. It is a Divine decree to stir the ingredients of love by making one offer a sacrifice. Sacrifice has always been love's ally.

Ulva's footsteps kept changing the amplitude of the echoes taking over the streets. Some steps sounded loud because a sudden thought would make her body go heavy, while the rest of the footsteps sounded damp because there was next to no energy left in her body. The more she kept getting close to the door, the more profusely she started to sweat. The night was finally ready for the reunion. She read the name on the board at the beginning of the street, it read *Revanche*. Now, her half-shut eyes were looking for a board that said 'House# 7'.

She was only a few steps away from the door she was expecting to knock at. Her feet were trying to resist her intentions to carry forward this journey, so she kept taking two steps back after every three steps. Tears hadn't stopped since she left the pharmacy. Somehow, she gathered her courage and climbed the stairs leading to the door. She was getting a feeling that the house was empty because there was no noticeable movement inside it. She saw the bell. She rang it multiple times but it didn't generate any sound. Finally, she decided to knock, but the fear and hesitation overpowered her knocks and they sounded too faint to give somebody any hint of a presence at the door. She stopped for a minute or two to catch her breath, because her heart felt sinking.

Finally, she did it the right way and knocked at the door properly. She did it for a while but there was no response. She was determined that the house was empty, and the mere thought of not witnessing the end made her stop sobbing. She felt a bubble bursting in her chest that was bearing all the intermediates to cause relish, but this happiness too didn't last long as fate was already on verge of revealing itself. One way or another, she would have to face it. The moment she turned around to leave the place, someone opened the door. She could feel the presence behind her, and just the thought of seeing him after so many years paralyzed her for a few seconds.

She could hear someone breathing heavily behind her. She decided to turn around and finally, her eyes caught a glimpse of the world's most pitiable being present at that time. She saw a young man looking way older than his age in utter disarray. The eyes made Ulva recognize him, it was Vernon. Her heart stopped beating for a second when she saw him in this condition.

> She kept whispering to herself, "I hadn't left him like this. Look what I have done!"

Vernon was looking more miserable than one could count as an extreme case. His clothes were worn out. His knees were bleeding, while the cloth of his trouser was sticking to his wounds as if it had merged into his skin. His chin, the corners of his lips, and his cheeks could be seen making way for the dripping blood. His hair was extremely dirty, as the oils were trapping a thick layer of dust on his scalp. His nose was runny. His clothes were covered in vomit and the smell was undoubtedly repulsive, but Ulva didn't care about anything. She only saw her son in front of her eyes whom she had given birth to. The bouquet fell on the ground, while she impulsively clasped her face between her hands out of despair. Tears were stuck in her eyes out of shock. Her eyes were wide open as if she couldn't believe what she was seeing. She knew that the reunion was going to be heart-wrenching, but the pain she was feeling at that moment was enough to kill her.

Vernon too had recognized the face of his mother. His half-shut eyes had become wide open by now. Seeing his mother, the first love of his life, in such a condition was unsurprisingly painful for him too. The mother she had always seen adorning all the charms being in such dreadful condition, hit him hard. Both of them had gotten frozen for a few moments. Their eyes greeted each other but their bodies were too weak to move even an inch.

After a few moments of silence, Ulva spoke with a quivering voice, "Vernon, is it you?"

She already knew the answer but she wanted him to say something. She was dying at that moment to hear his voice, but Vernon decided to stay silent. He started walking backward by taking small steps. The more he moved backward, the faster Ulva started to walk toward him. She heard a screeching sound in the house. It was the music player, but this too sounded sad to them.

Vernon turned around and rushed to the kitchen. He leapt towards the counter and grabbed a big sharp knife. Ulva was watching this with utter helplessness. She was expecting him to attack her.

He finally said just one word but repeated it thrice,

"Why? Why? Why?"

Ulva had started trembling again but with pain, not fear. She wanted to hug her son but the stretch of time wouldn't let them get any closer. Vernon swung his arm, the arm he was using to hold the knife, and brought the knife closer to his neck and slit his throat without even a single thought. Blood flowed out of his body with great pressure. He didn't even wait for a second to listen to his mother's explanation. Ulva fell to the ground, while Vernon fell on his knees too. She looked stunned as she was unable to comprehend the situation. Vernon fell in her lap, while she could see the deep cut in his neck filling her lap with blood. Her hands were trembling with greater intensity now, and she screamed with agonizing pain. Her wails were getting louder with each passing second. She couldn't take her eyes off Vernon's cut. The more she looked at it, the louder she screamed, and the screams broke every heart in the vicinity. Her screams could burst the sky, while the land would feel a tremble. All the metaphors became a reality that day. She gently brushed her fingers on the open edges of the cut. She wanted the ground to open itself and eat her up, but there was no way out of this.

The tale finally met an end after Vernon offered his sacrifice. Every other creature became teary-eyed, and their hearts kept bleeding after seeing this. Satan assumed this to be his victory, but he couldn't comprehend the lesson left behind as it preached love, not hate. Although the death of Vernon was unjust and he deserved every other happiness, but didn't everybody see that he had died the day he was left alone? His soul had already departed this world and now was his body. He was just waiting for his mother so he could sleep in her lap for the last time. No matter how things turned out before, a cycle somehow brought a mother and son together for the last time. Although this reunion couldn't last forever because everything has an end. The circumstances were unjust but this wasn't a loss at all. The wounds were deep for both of them, but the beauty of the relationship still made their heart melt with warmth. This was going to be remembered as a lesson and an unexplainable phenomenon, not a tragic end.

PART-II

A DUE APOLOGY & TRAIL OF REGRETS

THE SIXTH SYMBOL

I could never have imagined that I would meet you in such circumstances. Gaining you back and losing you at the very same time couldn't become any more soul-wrenching for me. No mother ever wants to hold her dead son in her lap, especially like this. Seeing you like this could have crumbled the mightiest mountain into ashes. I saw each drop of blood flowing out of your body until your body became completely hollow. I felt your warmth, I smelt your oddly familiar odor, and I felt your body that was holding your rattling bones together, and was lying like an open sack in my lap. You don't know how difficult it was for me to live everyday without you in Verrot, but my son, I had no other option. I did it for you, me, and Erasmus. I wish I could tell you the circumstances I left you in before you took your last breath. You can't imagine how alone I am. I am in more pain than anyone. I never got to see happiness in my life, but this can never justify the betrayal you had to face from my side. Even if I had reasons, I should have never left you. You know what? I was always ready to keep suffering for you, but seeing you suffer while seeing me suffer made everything more painful for me.

I kept caressing your hair and wiping your tears while your injured head sought refuge in my lap. You complained about your pains through your lifeless eyes. You left me alone in this meaningless world. But I don't have any right to complain now because you did what I did a decade ago. I am sorry my son. I never wanted to do this to you. I was so clueless that I couldn't weigh the after-effects of me leaving you like this. God has made the relationship of a mother and son so co-dependent that even the slightest hitch can make the entire universe tremble. Why wasn't it me instead of you lying on that floor, gasping for air? Why wasn't it me who would have to suffer from betrayal for all these years instead of you? Why did an innocent being like you had to be tested beyond his limits? I am sorry, I wish there was a sentiment that could describe my regrets and pain. I am lost, I am completely lost in this world. I don't know how to walk again. The only thing I can do is writing, just so an angel can deliver my message to you in heaven. I am the biggest sinner and I know my words won't make it to heaven, but God never rejects the plea of a mother.

I was counting every second in my home when I decided to travel all the way to meet you. I knew you weren't ok. I could feel the restlessness in my chest. I could feel that a part of me was missing and I somehow had to proclaim it back. But little did I know that I was going to lose you forever. Maybe I didn't lose you completely, but your presence would somehow be enough to keep me alive. I wish I could ask you to come back but then I remember your traumas, traumas that still get me chills and stab my heart every time I think about them. But still, why did you have to do this to yourself? Why did you hurt yourself for someone selfish like me? I don't deserve this sacrifice at all. A mother stays by her child's side until her last breath, but what did I do? I left you when you needed me the most.

My world started to crumble the day I saw your pictures on Dwayne's phone. I felt my soul escaping my body, while my heart tried its best to keep pumping blood. I lost all the colors of my life that day. I forgot to speak after seeing your worsening wounds. I wish those cuts had inflicted my body, and it should have been me feeling pain caused by those gruesome bruises. Do you know what broke my heart the most? That ring, the ring that I gave you before leaving. I couldn't forgive myself after the very moment I saw it on your injured fingers, because the ring was a reminder that you still somehow waited for me. My body was exhausted of energy after seeing that, but I still somehow gathered myself together and tried to reach you in one piece. Each part of my body was in agony, and I could feel my heart ripping into innumerable pieces and then clogging my veins. I could feel my brain going numb because I had lost everything. I was wrong. I miscalculated my moves and this is why you had to suffer from a betrayal like this. It was an uninvited and unwanted betrayal, but it still should have felt worse than any betrayal. I am sorry my poor child. This isn't a sorry for me to get forgiven, but for you to get some peace instead. You didn't deserve to ever feel that you weren't worth loving. You are the most beautiful thing that ever happened to me. I will meet you soon.

You don't know how cautious we would be with you when you were young. Dealing with a child with autism is an extra challenge, and keeping you safe was our priority. Erasmus and I mutually decided to homeschool you because we knew that the world was too overwhelming for you. Leaving you alone with strangers was the worst mistake that we ever wanted to make. Every moment spent with you became memorable in no time because you were a blessed kid. You never bothered us, nor did you make us feel the need for another child. You were our world. Erasmus used to love you too. We loved you equally. Seeing the moments you spent with him would be a sight of relish for me. The bond you two shared would make anybody gush with cherishment.

The night you left me, a destructive storm hit the city. The thunder was so loud that I had to hide in the guest room. I hid under the bed that you would like to play on. I was feeling scared and alone at the very same time. I knew it very well that there wasn't even a single familiar face left that could make me feel owned. I still remember that you would be terrified of thunderstorms. You would bury yourself in my arms while I would cover your head with my shawl. Just a few inches thick cloth associated with me would make you feel safe, even though the roars of agonizing thunder would still somehow make their way to your ears. An association of anything with me would make you feel safe. Why was I so stupid to forget that I was the only thing you needed in this world?

The funeral broke every attendee's heart. There were many recognizable faces, and everyone was eager to say their final goodbye to you. Every heart was feeling the pain of loss. There wasn't a single eye on the day that didn't shed tears. Even the birds and trees looked sorrowful. It seemed as if the colors were sucked out of everything in the premises of your casket. You looked handsome in the black suit. You told me once that black was your new favorite color when you discovered that black is pure in its own way. The bow tie hid the marks on your neck completely, and somehow made the whole proceedings manageable for me. I so wanted the land to open and suck me in. I was unable to withstand the sight of you lying lifeless in a casket. That is a parent's worst nightmare, burying their child with their own bare hands. Even animals find the pain of such loss insufferable. I am surprised at how I survived that evening. My nails still had dried blood clotted in their creases. Everything reminded me of you.

When I came back home after burying you, I tried to make myself fall asleep on the sofa in the lounge, but it felt as if I had forgotten how to sleep. My body was extremely fatigued from everything, but I was still unable to fall asleep. The uneasiness made me find my way to your room. Everything was in a disoriented situation. The bed cushion had deep cuts. The tables had been toppled and were lying upside down on the floor. The rocking chair of your father too had fallen sideways. The room felt colder than any other room in the entire house. The smell was stinky, but my senses slowly started getting numb the moment I saw the open drawers. It had a few letters. I walked slowly towards it. All of them were folded except the one lying open on the top of the table. The paper quality and the writing pattern looked different than the ones in the drawer. The letters were turning ashy as if even the slightest touch would make them conceal the words written on them. They had the number 41 written on their corners. I tried to configure the letters by checking the dates on them. I tried to decipher the meaning of the number 41 too. I somehow remembered the context of it but had forgotten the meaning. Then a glimpse at the blood-stained sheets of your bed reminded me of the talk we had related to the number, and I lost control of my body. I fell to the ground and started sobbing helplessly while hitting my head on the floor from despair. This number is a reminder of your past, of the past that I maligned with my existence.

On one 14th of February, you came to ask me about the significance of the day.

> "Mommy, what is 14th Feb for?" You asked with great innocence and curiosity.
> "Honey, you are too young to understand this but in short, this day is the one to proclaim your love for the ones that you desire to stay with forever."
> "Oh, just like I love you!"
> "Yes, dear!"

"Ok then, which day is for hatred? We surely hate many people."

"There isn't any day for it but if there were one, it could be 41st February," I replied jokingly while you chuckled because it didn't make any sense, but still delivered a message that was going to stay with us for quite some time. Just the flashback of your beautiful smile made me lose consciousness again.

Mr. Plankton gave me your diary. It was covered in blood stains, and once again, I lost a part of my existence after seeing the account of your pain. The diary has 41 engraved on it with a sharp object. There are multiple knife cuts on it. The diary has many torn pages but I still try to read it now and then. I didn't ask Mr.Plankton how he got his hands on this, but he has invited me for a talk. I have been delaying everything because I simply can't make sense of things going around me. I have forgotten who I am, what I want, and why I am here. I want to give your story closure, as I want to tell everyone how you were wronged and forced to become the unluckiest child ever born.

I have been hallucinating for the entire last week. It has been a while since I wrote the previous stuff. It was getting extremely difficult for me to pick up the pen again. I had zero courage to pen down your memories because even a simple reminiscence could kill me at any moment. I decided to read your diary but that too became unbearable after one point. I somehow managed to read those letters, and they were enough to shatter my heart. The words are still stuck in my mind, and the entire dialogue haunts me every night. There is a co-residing concern for Dwayne too because I haven't heard from him even once since he left. The feelings of remorse are killing me every second. I am constantly seeing our past in my dreams, and there is nothing that can make me forget it for a while. I guess this is what you get for betraying your loved ones.

THE REPLY TO HIS 'WHY?'

His hatred was inevitable and justified, but the way he said goodbye told me all the tales buried in his heart. He showed me the plan he had for himself for all this time. The determination he had in his eyes while taking his last breaths, made me realize that death was easier for him than suffering anymore. He was tired and it was time for him to leave his story to me for completion. Taking over his presence was the last thing that I ever wanted to do, but I had to swallow this bitter pill offered to me by destiny. We all know that we have no say in front of her because she is the one ruling all the emotions and ideologies in the chamber of untold truths. But I am destined to tell the truth of my existence too, so I must do it. Although I have gotten late, the lesson has to persist for centuries so now is better than later.

I never wanted to leave my family. A woman is expected by the society to keep her family intact, but it is her womanly instincts that compel her to make such sacrifices. She by nature does this, and gives up her peace for the sake of nourishing a new generation. Although this sounds and seems unfair and cruel, the inbuilt of their minds can never get unhinged. I was a content wife and mother, and I never felt as if I lacked anything in my life. Everything seemed perfect and went smoothly, as it was supposed to. Those random picnics with Vernon, the evening classes with him, and the bedtime stories, everything went as I always wanted it to. Even my life with Erasmus was very desirable at first. Though our marriage was arranged by my highly influential mother, I never felt that love was something that drove me bereft of him. The abrupt sessions of coitus: the curling of my back on the silk sheets, the heat from my rubbing heels making my body jolt with excitement, the brushing of my breasts against his chest, the peak of my orgasms while his moaning grunts would get whispered in my ears, the sweat from his groin making my labia more wet, and his gentle strokes that would make me bury my nails deeper into his hairy back, everything would feel empyreal. I didn't have anything to complain about, and thus, I was satisfied with the life I had with him until one point.

If I were told two decades ago that I would be the one leaving my family alone in a few years, I would have shunned the claims immediately, as I used to believe that there was nothing that could go wrong enough to compel me to take such a decision. But it didn't take long to make me realize that I was wrong. It all happened that one day, the day when the hue surrounding our abode felt dense. Nothing seemed different at first until I got to interact with Erasmus. His attitude seemed stern. He sounded unapologetically cold, taunted me for things that were never my fault, and started reminding me of all the mistakes I had made in my life till that day. This attitude became our new companion. The bitterness and harshness in his tone would make me cry over my misery every other day. I couldn't force myself to stay content with my life after that day. I kept ignoring these red flags. I kept trying to make him change, but everything seemed off. It felt as if I wasn't enough for him. I was told by my instincts that Erasmus had already given up on the vows of monogamy that we had proclaimed on our wedding day, but I kept trying to make myself stay gracious. I had no other option but to stay for Vernon. Life was already difficult for him, and I didn't want him to get under the dark influence of this inevitable truth involving our broken marriage.

I tried justifying Erasmus's every move to myself,

but I reached a limit after some time. This had to happen eventually because now the security of Vernon's future was at stake. There wasn't a chance that I would hurt him just to get myself relished with this thought, that I had him and he had me. The mere thought of me being close to him was proving disastrous. Thus, I had to weigh my steps and plan my future. A future that was more about Vernon than me. A future that was going to be less bleak than my forgotten past.

I was constantly told by Dwayne that Erasmus didn't deserve me. He kept telling me that I should have left him the day he abused me for the first time. That slap didn't just jerk my body, it made my soul shiver. It cracked the window in my heart that opened to the corridors leading to the remains of Erasmus's existence. These remains always held meaningful importance for me because they would keep me going. Although it was just the remains that had been residing in my heart, not his entire existence, because his first push to shake my existence happened to occur on my wedding day.

While I was getting ready for my special day, he brought me a dress that was his mother's. We had already mutually bought a lavish white gown, but the constant insistence of his mother made him enforce her liking on me. When I refused, he pushed me, held me by my arms, and threw me across the room with all the power he had. He lost the respect I had for him that day, and thus it was the broken heart I had been carrying with me since then.

That first slap too didn't happen quite long after we got married. Although his care for me never lacked, the unexpected episodes of rage would often strike me with fear. I would try to avoid him in such situations, but one day it seemed impossible to me to ignore his existence. I had to stand against him, and thus the repercussion I had to face was a merciless slap. My tears were clinging to the shore of my eyes and they wouldn't breach the boundaries at all, because the fear of getting hit again had made me forget my entire existence. My say, my presence, and my honor held no value at that time, thus I couldn't even grieve properly. I escaped the house temporarily the moment I got the chance. My hand rested on my bruised cheek for the whole time, while I ran barefoot in the street, and somehow I unwantedly reached Dwayne's pharmacy. His eyes too looked stunned with shock when he saw me in such a situation. He tried to console me even though I wasn't crying, instead, I wasn't even blinking out of shock. I was stiff as if I had already become hollow inside. Dwayne gently draped me in his coat, while I was unable to feel even the slightest warmth around me. My senses had become numb. He kept looking into my eyes while I looked into his, and then, he started whimpering immediately. He looked distressed after seeing me like this, while my hand was still stiffly covering my bruised cheek. He just did not see my pitiful body shivering with disbelief and heartbreak, but he felt my pain too.

After sitting close to each other for a few minutes, the warmth radiating out of his body made me feel less uneasy, and I removed my hand from my cheek. The moment he saw my wounded face, his eyes became wide open while tears kept rolling down his cheeks relentlessly. His lips seemed to twitch as if he wanted to say something, but didn't have any energy to do so. He gently moved closer to me, brought his hand near my face, and touched my face delicately while his eyes gave me an apologetic look. His gentleness and care made me realize that there were still some desired souls out there. Seeing his distressed situation made me forget my pain, and I impulsively held his hand and squeezed it tightly. I leaned towards his body and placed my head in his lap. He hesitatingly caressed my hair and rubbed the back of my neck with his warm and smooth fingers. I kept weeping silently while he kept gazing at my wounds, alas, he couldn't see the wounds in my heart. My heart was in more pain than my body, and he didn't know that somehow unintentionally, he was healing my wounds. The gentler his strokes on my arms started to get, the more I kept falling for him.

I fell in love with him. A man can undo the damage done by another man. I raised my body, matched his stature, and leaned toward his lips. I looked into his eyes and they were giving me a sense of acceptance. His breath kept tingling the ridges on my lips, and the papillae kept oozing moisture to soften my lips as if nature was already ready to accept our love. I kissed him gently and left the pharmacy. I walked a few feet away when he called me by my name. I stopped immediately but didn't turn around.

> "If you don't want to go back to your house, you can stay for the night at mine." His voice sounded softest of all the times I had heard him. I didn't respond for a minute, and then I turned around.
> "Sure," I replied with a quivering voice.

That night was the one when I lost my whole identity as Erasmus's wife. My heart, my soul, and my body accepted Dwayne as my soul mate. The moments we spent together, stayed with me forever. Although I had to hide them somewhere unseen in my brain at one point, I never denied this claim that I loved him, even more than Erasmus. That night was one of the most beautiful nights that I ever got to witness, and with the blessings of it, I conceived Vernon. He was the son of the love of my life.

The news of my pregnancy changed my life. Erasmus started acting differently with me. He was being the best version of himself. After the day I got pregnant, I didn't get to witness his rage for quite a while. Those days were the best ones of my life. I had everything that I desired. I had a loving husband, a son who was about to be born, and a comfortable life. Things seemed to get better for me, and I always felt obliged because it was Dwayne who helped me with them. He was the savior of my present. Although I had to give up on what I had with him, I knew that he wanted my happiness. He wasn't like the selfish ones who go to any extent to get what they have to. He genuinely tried to improve my life, and waited for me. Although the wait was a long shot, he did it.

The day Vernon was born and the final push that welcomed him into our lives, everything made me forget my ugly past with Erasmus. I started a new chapter, a new life, and I literally felt better than ever. Everything seemed different than before. I became completely content with what I had after giving birth, and never even got second thoughts. Erasmus became completely mine and till Vernon's 12th birthday, Erasmus never even dared to talk to me harshly, so hitting me was out of question. We lived a life that made everyone around us envious. We took care of our autistic kid with all our energy, and this was the most beautiful part of my life: staying close to Vernon and being there for him.

But, there was an expiry date for this artificial period of happiness. One evening, we were driving back from the grocery store when over a small debate, Erasmus started getting aggressive. It was the time when he had already started acting cold. The heat of the moment didn't even get me a chance to retreat. He held me stiffly from the lock of my hair, and twisted his hand, while the aggressive pull of each and every strand of my hair drove me to the verge of me screaming with pain and breaking into tears. He used his other hand to punch me below my right eye. Vernon stepped in and tried to stop Erasmus. He kept sobbing and trembling with fear, but he still decided to intervene. I tried to send him away but he wouldn't go. Erasmus was hit by some realization and he immediately stopped.

This continued for a while. Most of the time it would happen behind the closed doors. Vernon wouldn't have even the slightest idea of what I would go through. Erasmus would pull me by my locks and would swing my head, eventually smashing it against a wall. He would push me around the room with his merciless thrusts. This continued for a while and I kept hiding it from Vernon. To him, his apparent father was still a hero. Little did Erasmus know that Dwayne was

Vernon's actual father, but the relationship Vernon had with him would sometimes make me feel safe. Although I used to suffer every day, I would look up to Vernon's smiling face, and would push away all the thoughts stirring a sense of disappointment in my existence. I kept going for him, and it was him later who made me leave everything behind forever.

Then something unexpected happened and I had to abandon the thoughts of leaving. Erasmus fell down the stairs and got half-paralyzed. Some of the happy moments I had spent with him in the past, and Vernon, made me willingly accept this fate for me, and I happily took care of an abusive husband like Erasmus. I stayed with him until I could.

But even then, Erasmus's repulsive attitude didn't change. Even after being unable to abuse me physically, he wouldn't let go of any chance to torture me mentally. The taunts, the shouts, and the verbal abuse, everything would make me want to die from disgrace. By now, Vernon too had started witnessing things, and it was becoming too much for a kid like him. I had the option to make him feel less burdened, and thus I decided to finally opt for it.

Dwayne was already secretly aware of our situation. Garth had become a part of our family by then, and out of pity, he had told Dwayne everything to protect me. Dwayne would hesitate to see me every time I would go to the pharmacy, just to make it feel less burdening for me. He later confessed that the love he had for me wouldn't allow him to see me suffering. But this too lasted for a short while, as we decided to leave the city for good.

I had already prepared the divorce documents. I made Erasmus sign the papers before I left. While I was signing them, I got many second thoughts, but then I saw Vernon's innocent face and signed them immediately. Erasmus only hated me, but his love for Vernon was unshared and unexplainable, so it was best to leave Vernon with Erasmus.

The day I had to leave Onerwaarten was difficult too. Vernon was sleeping in his bed peacefully as if he had no worries in his life. I didn't want him to get impacted by any worries too. I sat beside his bed for half an hour and kept kissing his small hands. It was about time for him to wake up. I quickly moved my bags to the door. I kissed him gently on his forehead and left with tears. That walk was the most painful for me. The farther I kept walking away from his room, the more painful and sore my arms and legs were becoming. Ultimately, I had to gulp down my tears and leave Onerwaarten with Dwayne.

Dwayne proposed to me on our way, and we got

married in Verrot. There was not a single day when I didn't think of Vernon. Thus, his hate for me is justified, but the final moments that I spent with him showed me that he too was stuck in a dilemma, the one caused by the ongoing war between love and hatred. Hatred made him leave me without giving me the chance to explain myself, and love made him give his sacrifice by protecting me from all the suffering. He took everything on himself instead of taking out his anger on me, or anyone else. This is why I call him the most virtuous human I have ever seen. No action of his could be wrong enough to get him declared guilty, because he was the forgiven one. His sufferings make his mistakes look bleak and non-existent.

I lost him just like he lost me once, but I am determined that we will reunite again, and then me and Dwayne will stay by his side forever.

THE FINALE OF THE TALE

THE SECOND SYMBOL

It all was an illusion. Mr. Plankton called on me yesterday to discuss some very depressing information. I had hardly started to make sense of things, and then this revelation shattered me completely. Everything seems to have gotten stuck in a trapped dungeon. I find myself abandoned in it too because things are happening, and I am unable to get hold of any of them. There are so many regrets that are keeping me entangled in these creeping ivies. I hope this is it for now and I get time to process everything.

I couldn't sleep after meeting Mr. Plankton. His words still haunt me in my dreams, and my days seem to have turned into a nightmare by them. I had never imagined that one heartbreak would prove this fatal and disastrous for everyone.

The walk to Mr. Plankton's house was very difficult. My heart was palpitating. When I reached his door, it was open. I knocked twice but there was no response. I entered the house without waiting any further. He was sitting on a wooden chair while gazing at the floor. He looked worried and sick. I wasn't in a position myself to ask him about his pale appearance and trembling hands. He was having a hard time breathing too. His eyes were turning yellow. He looked weaker than when I had seen him at the funeral. I walked hesitatingly towards him. I sat on the chair next to him and tried to start a conversation. The mutual loss was bothering both of us, and it was getting difficult to hold up a conversation related to Vernon. But no matter what, we had to talk to figure some stuff out.

He started by telling me about Vernon's cheerful personality. He talked about how great of a human Vernon was. We both agreed that he was the strongest human we both ever knew. I was unable to control my tears, and it was getting more difficult for me to swallow them with each passing minute. He told me about how Vernon seemed to be doing just fine at first. To him, he used to seem happy. He mentioned something about his wife, Willa too.

I read about his marriage in the diary. I was feeling

so calm and happy to read about the love of his life, and how she had filled the void for him. I kept reading about her, but there was an abrupt ending to the account. Many pages were missing in the book. After every chapter, there were tear marks. I first thought that it was Vernon who had torn those pages. In his childhood, he would frequently tear some of the pages from his diary because he wouldn't be satisfied with the way they would turn out. I didn't seem to pay much notice and completed reading the whole diary while sulking.

Mr. Plankton kept talking after taking small breaks as he was trying to be sensitive with his words. He would give me tissues in between with his shaky hands because I was constantly weeping. He tried to make it as easy as possible, but after all, the discussion was about the most lovable asset of my life, so I couldn't hold it anymore. He started telling me about his sudden trip to Vernon's house. Then he talked about the queer things that happened at the house.

> "I was supposed to meet his wife. He was ready to make me meet her, but something disturbing happened after that," he said with a soft tone.
> After a few seconds pause, I managed to ask, "What was it?"
> "I never got to meet Willa. He kept calling her but there was nobody. When it started to get late, he got a panic attack and things got

excruciatingly painful for both of us."
"What do you mean by that? She must have left the house for something. I read so much about her in the diary." I stopped sobbing for a while and asked him with great concern.
"Well you read about her but where is she now? There was no mention of her leaving him at any moment. I stole his diary after breaking into his house. I read everything and—" Mr. Plankton stopped after that.

I was extremely stunned after hearing this. His every word was stinging me. His cautiously uttered words wanted to reveal a bitter truth to me but I was intentionally trying to ignore all the possible details.

> "Look, Mrs. Dwayne. I am so sorry for your loss, I truly am, but you have to believe me too. The things I am going to tell you now are what I concluded after analyzing everything I could lay my hands on." He continued telling me in his weak voice.

I was feeling petrified and stupefied before any of the confessions because I wasn't ready to hear anything bad at all. I wasn't ready for any news, any revelation, or any detail that could haunt me forever. But time couldn't get any crueler. It had to happen someday and it did. I was eventually hit by a gigantic boulder that made me black out immediately. Mr. Plankton started his series of revelations.

> "Vernon was in extreme pain a few weeks before his death. I would visit him often and he was in the worst condition. His body used to be always drenched in blood. I am sorry if it is difficult for you to hear this and I shouldn't tell you, but he was in more pain than you can imagine. He was completely devastated. Death was the only treatment for him—" He stopped here because I had started gasping, and he had to witness a meltdown of a devastated and lonely mother.

We stayed quiet for a few minutes, and then I tried to make him tell me everything. I was finally ready to get done with it.

> "I am sorry, I haven't been feeling like myself recently, and things are very difficult for me. You can tell me everything. I am genuinely relieved that you cared about him and that now you want to tell me about his condition."
> "I can completely feel your loss. I will try to make it sound as less painful as possible." His tone was melancholic now.
> He continued, "The few nights before his death, his body was suffering from extreme insomnia. He was getting seizures and multiple psychotic attacks, so I had to inject him with some medicines to relieve his pain. This would make him sleep peacefully for a few hours, otherwise, things could have gotten worse for him. I had

already sensed his deteriorating condition from the diary so I found it necessary to help him out," he took a small pause once again, and then completed his talk, "the day I had to meet Willa was the one when I had started doubting his mental condition. He was clearly schizophrenic. Everything became more crystal clear when I read his diary."

By now, his eyes had started to get filled with tears. I too wept with him. Then it began to rain, and the atmosphere turned more sad and painful than we expected it to. The sound of raindrops hitting the top of the roof was reminding me of my mental condition. But still, I was listening to Mr. Plankton attentively as I didn't want to miss even a single detail.

"The diary was written from two perspectives. One-half of the diary was written by Vernon as Willa. She supposedly wrote the diary in first-person and tried to explain Vernon's behavior. It was shocking for me at the beginning because I was unable to comprehend anything at all. Then when I read about her being diagnosed as a schizophrenia patient by Vernon, I immediately realized that it was him who had the disorder," he took a tissue close to his eyes and wiped his tears, and then continued, "I know it is too much for you to hold right now, but let me explain my deduction. There are multiple instances where schizophrenia patients suffer from dissociative disorder too. Here, the patient has multiple personalities and in Vernon's case, Willa was his other personality." He had started panting while explaining everything.

My mouth was wide open out of shock and disbelief after he told me the name of Vernon's illness. I kept looking at him with my grieving eyes, while he looked back at me with a look of reassurance. I held the arm of my chair tightly because the room had started to spin in front of my eyes. After I came back to my senses, I asked him to complete the conversation. He too wanted to complete this talk as soon as possible.

"I read the entire diary and burnt a portion of it. I know I shouldn't have stepped in but I wanted to protect Vernon. This was the best way I could think of. There were many things that he had discussed and they needed a burial. For example, Willa called herself Dwayne's daughter and wrote multiple times that Vernon wanted to hurt her to seek revenge. She also wrote about how Vernon was trying to paralyze her and drive her insane. Things were getting incomprehensible with each increasing chapter so I tried to go through them at my own pace —," he took a long breath and then said, "I was completely lost after reading one of the chapters. In that, he wrote from Willa's perspective and confessed that he murdered Garth. The reason wasn't mentioned but the details were. I couldn't think of anything besides burning it to safeguard him from any more suffering."

I fell from the chair immediately as it was getting unbearable for me. Mr. Plankton tried to make me stand again but he looked too fragile to do so. I tried to hold myself together but I was falling apart. Now, everything seemed to make sense in true aspects. Those random texts and images sent to Dwayne were Vernon's way of informing that he was seeking revenge in his mind, but my poor boy, oh my poor boy, he didn't know that he was hurting himself only.

I used all of my energy to leave the room and ran towards my house. I shut the door with great force because I was dying from the crushing pain these confessions were causing. I kept praying to call the angel of death but nothing seemed to work. I wanted to die immediately because these daunting memories were enough to make my guilt weigh more. A single betrayal by me had done so much damage that multiple lives were put at stake. Two kids lost their father because of me. This couldn't get any more agonizing.

There was silence for two weeks in my life. I had all this time for myself to gulp down everything that I had discovered, but I can't understand why it won't stop now. I was happy and sad at the very same time thinking that this tale had already ended, but it didn't take me long to realize that it was just the beginning. I hope this beginning is the new end.

Garth's sister-in-law Shayna came back. Yesterday morning, she knocked at my door and was surprised to see me inside. She seemed furious at first and was not ready to talk to me, and insisted on meeting Vernon. Her tone was assertive but harsh. I tried to tell her about his death, but it was getting difficult for me to control myself.

> After she kept insisting, I blurted out, "He is dead! What do you want now? Let him have some peace!"

> There was a shock in her eyes. She seemed to have gotten stuck in a brief moment of disbelief. She looked into my eyes and said, "I am sorry for what happened," she paused and reached inside her trench coat and took out a folded letter, "This is the last letter that Garth wrote. I found it in the kids' items. I thought it could help us with finding out about his death, but now, it is meaningless to investigate any further." Her tone was sympathetic this time.

I moved my hand forward but my fingers felt stiff. I somehow managed to take that paper from her hand. She left immediately after that. I kept looking at her walking till she disappeared in the street. I got back in. I stared at the folded paper for a while, and then decided to open and read it. During this whole time, I tried to control my nerves and read the whole letter in one go.

Greetings everyone,

I am writing this as a memoir and strictly forbid everyone from using it as an evidence to dig into something. If things have become this complicated that you are reading this letter, I do realize that the circumstances must have gotten very crucial and excruciating for Vernon too. This is me trying to connect to my two munchkins and everyone who cared about me. I know this letter reaches one hand at a time, so right now, I am addressing YOU.

My life was beautiful with my family. I never felt the need for parents because I had Erasmus and Ulva. They took care of me just like Vernon. My needs were prioritized, and I will be always thankful to them. The things they did for me are priceless, and that's why I owe them a lot. I want Vernon to live a happy and peaceful life even if it makes me the one leaving my kids behind. I know they will be loved even without me, so I have no complaints. Instead, I will be the one who is going to remain stuck in the sucking mud of guilt.

I was disloyal because I somehow used unfair

and heinous means to gain the love of my life. I went astray, and I will always regret doing this. I ended everything with my own hands. I am the one responsible for Vernon's condition, and he shouldn't be blamed at all. I took his father away from him. Lord, what was I thinking while doing it?

I can never forget the days when I was plotting murder with Dwayne. I was so blinded by love that I couldn't distinguish between it and hate. I deserve zero sympathy, and I want none, to be honest. I am happy with having two wonderful kids who will leave their legacy. I regret not giving them the life they deserved, but time is so cruel, everything happens fast, and you don't even get to grasp the magnitude of destruction you are causing. There is a ripple effect that somehow connects everything. It brings back your evil deeds to hit back at you, sooner or later. The very same thing happened to me. I am the one behind this broken and doomed Vernon. I took away his liveliness, and I deserve to get punished for it. It isn't just now that I am realizing my mistakes, I have been cursing myself since the day I messed with the balance of life and death.

Vernon had started showing signs of schizophrenia right after Erasmus's death. He locked himself in the house for a week, and we didn't get to hear anything from him during that period. After one week, we saw him at the pharmacy in a wretched condition. His eyes were serving to be the doors for the dark and empty corridors extending inside his body.

After a few months, he told us about his marriage. Everyone was shocked. None of us was invited. He told us about the details and all of us were happy for him, but confused too. It didn't take me long to realize that there was something up with him. I stayed silent for weeks. I kept observing his behavior. Within a month, his behavior started to make me suspect that he was schizophrenic.

After a year or two, he started taking medicines for Willa. He told us that she was experiencing hallucinations. We tried to convince him to visit the hospital, but he kept disagreeing. He would tell us that Willa was petrified of stepping out into the world. We would pretend to believe him, but everyone was worried about his situation.

After another few months, his hallucinations started to get worse. I finally decided to slowly tell him about his illness, but he would ignore everything, so I stopped bothering him much. After some time, he began to act aggressively. One time, he threw a glass bottle on my head when I tried to convince him to get checked for any disorder. I knew he meant no harm, but I was worried about his condition. He was daily taking schizophrenia-related medicines from the pharmacy for Willa. Things worsened when he started taking diazepam too. It is a sedative injection used in surgeries. I never dared to ask him what he would use it for, but I was alarmed at his condition.

This continued until I decided to convince him to visit a doctor. Mr. Plankton was long gone too, so there was no one whom I could trust. I didn't want him to end up at a mental asylum because he didn't deserve it. This dilemma continued for a while. I still can't figure out a way to stop his illness from worsening.

It is already too late, and the only thing I can do is take good care of him by helping him deal with this. We can sense his uneasiness and pain. He looks disheveled these days, and it hurts me that I can't do anything about it. Why is it that we only get left with regrets while the damage is already done? Why don't we get any second chances or warnings? I could have stopped it, but now I can't. This is how I repaid someone for their care and affection. I hope my kids turn out differently, and I hope they try to shape this world into a better place where people realize the grave seriousness of betrayal, and how it can crumble the whole world into ashes.

I am sorry Ulva if you ever read this letter, but this is a way of me proving Vernon's innocence.

He just tried to protect his existence because there was nobody else to lend him a helping hand. He was left alone after what we all did to him. I hope you forgive me. I can't see Vernon surviving for much longer because of his already deteriorating condition, but I hope his last breaths serve a sense of purpose for many going through the same trauma. I wish I could fix everything but I can't. Whoever is reading this letter, please take good care of my kids. Do tell them that I miss them. I hope their lives help many people like Vernon.

Written with a broken heart,
Garth

Confessions are rare to come across in a world like this, but love makes you confess. Forgiveness stirs love in the surroundings. The letter was gut-wrenching for me to read because it brought back all the memories, but I finally got a hint from nature that this is the ending of Vernon's story. His sufferings finally found words. Now, his soul must be resting peacefully in the heavenly abode. Everything was distressing for me too, but I had a lesson to propagate, and through my mistakes, I know many Ulvas will realize the importance of an uninterrupted show of affection.

On the other hand, it is also important to

realize that love and hatred are what make this world a real test, and everybody makes unique choices to make this life different for them. My mistakes can be the only option for someone else, and this is how multiple stories generate a bedazzling and bewitching halo effect. We mostly tend to underestimate hatred. It is the only thing that makes two lovers split eventually, taking everything in the surroundings in its wrath. In our story, the wrath took Vernon from us. I had to make certain difficult decisions, and there was a great chance of destruction accompanying them, but I did everything I could as a mother. I wasn't the best mother, but I prioritized my son over everything. My sacrifices are nothing but mere obligations that I fulfilled, but some might see them as a reason to applaud me and declare me a hero. Therefore, motherhood is a crucial pillar to the peace of this world. It is a relationship that adds softness and intricacies to the diffusing array of emotions.

However, Vernon too made us all learn an important lesson. He told everyone that if you have no one, be your own partner. You can never betray and leave yourself, and this is how you don't end up completely deserted even if everyone seems to be gone.

The Satan-spurred war met a temporary and unconventional end this time, but there is going to be a decisive moment when millions of stories will resonate to bring him down. Till then, love is the only way to stand upright because we have to protect millions of Vernons.

PART-III

THE 7 SYMBOLS

CONCLUDING LINES FOR THE EXPERIMENT:

(I, Dr. Plankton, pledge that I will work till my last breath to help out the ones that are in search of a beacon of hope. I will do everything to share their pain, and make them feel owned)

Humans are capable of doing great damage. This experiment proved it. We don't often realize that even the most common step taken by a person capable of hurting others, can shake the entire universe, eventually generating a loop of havoc that can cause suffering to an inhumane extent. Humans hurting humans is becoming a massive problem, and this is why we conducted this experiment. Common pains can trigger similar emotions, thus shaping a tale that is common to all, as we saw in this case.

Vernon and Ulva were amongst the notable writers of their time. They were revered for the work and the impact that it generated. They are still remembered by many, but their sudden disappearance has been a mystery for many. Little does everyone know that the constant torture led by fellow humans was what made such successful personalities encounter a tragic end. Vernon and Ulva are the literal tragic heroes of this story. Both of them suffered from similar pains, thus tailoring a similar tale. Both of them ended up in mental asylums because of predictable, but heartbreaking betrayals. Both of them had the capability to revolutionize this world with their words, but Satan made them fall into a pit that was dug by their loved ones, the ones who never bothered to reciprocate such priceless emotions with appropriate expressions. My heart bleeds when I write a conclusion for their story.

I very carefully took this responsibility to narrate the messages extracted from their lives just to reach the masses with a lesson intended to bring a change: a lesson about the wonders of love, and the evils of hatred. Betrayals are inevitable and they are in human nature, but the disastrous outcomes can be tackled with necessary preparations. I am quite convinced that the lesson was intricately withdrawn. Now, I have to conclude this emotionally draining process with great sensitivity.

To sum it up for everyone invested in this experiment, I have to tell them that Ulva and Vernon never had a physical connection. It was the psychological connection that made them communicate in a way that they came up with a similar story just to get their trauma some words. They showed us that hatred affects everyone in the same way, and that love has to prevail, especially self-love. Both of them forgot the importance of self-love and somehow got carried away by the fierce waves of life, thus, they deemed it necessary to join us in this mission to propagate a positive message by making everyone learn from their mistakes and sufferings.

Vernon was Samantha's only child. She left him with his paralyzed father at a very young age. She abandoned them for materialistic gains and never looked back for years. She got married to someone rich, and then adopted a son. Vernon's father took great care of him, but later succumbed to his past injuries. Until his father's death, Vernon wrote many novels about spirituality. His words had started to resonate with the thoughts of his readers right at the beginning of his career, and he eventually earned the title that declared him a revolutionary writer. But this lasted for a short period. His mental health began to deteriorate after his father's death. He was clearly unable to manage the grief and started suffering from schizophrenic episodes. He suffered for a while, and eventually, his condition took an unexpected turn. His mother came back after her second husband's death, but when Vernon got to confront her, he couldn't make sense of his surroundings, and these complications made him attack her with a knife, leaving her with severe wounds. He was sent to our mental asylum, and since then, I have been personally taking care of him.

On the other hand, Ulva was married to Erasmus. She was in love with him. However, her marriage was traumatic from the beginning. She wouldn't complain at all about her husband's violent blows. The abuse continued till the very last date of her marriage. While she was in hope of getting loved by her chosen companion, she used to write many romantic novels that made her earn a great name among the masses. Her books were called *Exquisitely Magical* by the critics. She kept writing until she had to face something heartbreakingly tragic. She was 7 months pregnant with a boy when Erasmus abused her to the extent that she got a miscarriage. After the miscarriage, she was in a state of trance over losing her son. She had lost her will to live, and she started suffering from an extreme case of depression. She was later diagnosed with multiple personality disorder too. She made multiple attempts to kill Erasmus, and eventually, he left her here, and thus this is how we got to listen to her painful story.

This story about Vernon and Ulva in general is a perfect depiction of the fact that wounds left by betrayal are difficult to heal, and the suffering that it causes shows no anomaly or variation. We opted for this experiment after consultation with many medical boards, and with the consent of both of these humble personalities. Finally, we made them write a tale capturing their traumas in a different way. We were shocked to discover that even if the writers had independent gut-wrenching pasts, they came up with a completely cohesive story. Both of the written stories fitted together like a jigsaw puzzle, while I just played the role of filling the empty spaces.

As expected, both of them wrote about the possible expectations from love, and how they were left deprived of this emotion. This process was emotionally challenging for Ulva and Vernon, but they tried to cooperate as much as they could. We didn't force them to write more than their capacities, thus, the purity in their souls reflected in the story that they told. I am relieved that the Divine help made me delicately carry this whole account while deducing the possible lessons from the symbols hidden in their lives. Their stories intricately followed the true definition of symbolism, thus making us victorious in our mission.

The 7 symbols were intentionally added to the tale to amplify the message. The interaction of Ulva with Samantha, the appearance of Willa, the kid murderer, the swan that sacrificed itself, the animal form of Aphrodite, 41, and the mourning peacock, every single symbol served a purpose. 41, the symbol of hate, ruled the rest of the symbols, thus dominating the most. Hatred was the constant theme that led to so much suffering, and that's why this experiment was named after it.

Starting with the first symbol, the interaction of Samantha and Ulva symbolized how different of mothers both of them were. One of them lost her sanity after losing her child, while the other one hurt her only child just to satisfy her lust for wealth. This symbol balanced love and hate for both of the mothers. The conversation they had, played a focal role in infusing the existence of both characters in order to draw a lesson.

Moving further, Willa (Vernon's illusionary personality) symbolized the need for self-love. Her existence showed that Vernon had lost everything except himself. He had found solace in his own personality and existence. Even if it was an illusion, it served the purpose to support him through thick and thin when he had lost everyone around him. The moment when he stopped finding Willa around himself, symbolized that he had become spiritually dead after how things kept turning out for him. He lost the reason to live, and thus, he lost himself too. This left a message that how self-love can stop you from losing yourself. Even if you think that you are left alone and things seem to be ending, you can be your own savior.

On the other hand, the kid murderer represented Dwayne's story where he had deprived a kid of his liveliness. It necessarily meant the person whom Samantha had gotten married to, because he had somehow deprived Vernon of his childhood. He had lured Samantha, resulting in driving a mother and a son apart. Dwayne as an individual in this story was his representation, thus the symbol served the purpose to shed light on his sins.

Furthermore, the sacrificial swan represented Vernon's bleak future. It showed the fact that he had been left alone by the people in his surroundings, and eventually, he had to halt the continuity of his existence. The sequence where he ran while getting hurt, symbolized that he had run a long way while being controlled by his surroundings. His choices no longer mattered because people around him weren't giving him a chance to do something for himself. He had gotten tired of the painful run, eventually finding peace with the fact that he had to end everything. So he gradually prepared himself to give up because he had failed to keep up with the standards set for him.

The fifth symbol, the animal form of Aphrodite, summarized Ulva's feelings and her ugly past. It explained how she had to face betrayal at her husband's hand. The tale epitomized the sacrifices she had made to keep her marriage going. The attack she had to get impacted by in the dream, symbolized Erasmus's aggressive nature. The continuous mental and physical abuse she was suffering from, got to find its own words in this symbol to commend Ulva for the sacrifices she had made.

The mourning peacock got to be another symbol chosen in honor of Ulva's courageous sacrifices, especially the sacrifice she had made by losing her child. The events drawn in that tale went hand in hand with what Ulva had to go through while giving up on her child. The way that mother lost her child, resonated with Ulva's story of miscarriage which she was holding on to for the last few years.

Thus each symbol got its own set of explanations to complete the tale for Ulva and Vernon. The symbols were a necessity to appropriately convey each emotion that both of them had gone through. It won't be wrong to say that symbol 41 controlled this whole story, and then fragmented into further symbols. Hatred is a pain giver, and this is a given fact. Love is to neutralize it, but sometimes it is difficult to find it. Seeking love from others in some instances seems impossible, so the only way to deal with everything is to love yourself. It is also important to realize that the ones suffering aren't alone as there are millions of others that encounter similar emotions, because the stimuli triggered after going through all this presents a similar trend. Suffering can never get halted, but the way it impacts one, it has to be addressed. It is important to make everyone realize how great of a threat self-harm is to the universe. The pain has to be shared with others to infuse a sense of realization in general. I hope one day people realize that the lives of other people hold the same importance as their own. The world seems to be more hatred driven than anything else, but I am determined that this phenomenon is soon going to lose its hold.

This is Dr. Plankton signing off with deepest regards for everyone who helped us conduct this experiment, especially the two brave souls: Vernon and Ulva.

THE END

ACKNOWLEDGEMENT

First thanks to God Almighty for giving me the courage to complete this book. It was an arduous task but with His will, I concluded my work on a beautiful note. He has filled my life with some wonderful presences and that's why I was able to do what I was always destined for. My mother and father, the combined beacon of determination, somehow enabled me to capture my feelings in this novel appropriately. Ali Saiem Chaudhary and Mohibullah Amir, my tremendously wonderful friends' unwavering support made me lead this work to a heartfelt point. I am overwhelmed in all humbleness and gratefulness to acknowledge my depth to all those who have helped me to put these ideas, well above the level of simplicity and into something concrete.

I deem myself to be a lucky guy for channeling my emotions and sufferings intricately to generate a solid piece that will become a lesson of hope for many.

I would also like to express my special thanks of gratitude to my teacher, Sir Muhammad Jameel, who encouraged me at every point of my student life. This book is dedicated to all the kind souls that are playing their role in making this world a better place.

ABOUT THE AUTHOR

Muhammad Irtiza Mehdi

M. Irtiza Mehdi is a medical student. He is Pakistan's first psychological-thriller novelist in English. He achieved this feat at a young age. He started writing at the age of 16 and debuted at the age of 18. He has always taken a keen interest in addressing many problems in the society. He has shed light on numerous crucial issues in the past, whether it be awareness about some disease, or some social cause, for instance, honor killings. He has been vocal about his struggles for a while, thus he wants to make it easier for others. After being a victim of barbaric bullying since childhood, he decided to talk about it and leave an impact. He believes that talking against misogyny, patriarchy, and toxic masculinity will stir an environment of self-awareness. This book is one of his steps toward achieving his goal.

For queries and remarks, contact on this email: mirtiza1413@gmail.com

Printed by Amazon Italia Logistica S.r.l.
Torrazza Piemonte (TO), Italy